코끼리

바이링궐 에디션 한국 대표 소설 049

Bi-lingual Edition Modern Korean Literature 049

The Elephant

김재영

코끼리

Kim Jae-young

ASIA
PUBLISHERS

Contents

코끼리

The Elephant

시월이 되자 아버지는 한길로 향한 창문에 퍼체우라
(네팔 남자들이 몸에 걸치는 직사각형의 천)를 쳤다. 틀이 일
그러진 바라지창 틈새로 스며드는 밤안개에 아버지가
심하게 기침을 한 다음날이었다. 지난여름, 장판 밑에
서 시작된 곰팡이는 방바닥에 놓인 세간과 벽에 걸린
옷가지로 번져나가더니 기어코 아버지의 폐와 내 종아
리까지 점령했다. 아버지는 기침을 해댔고 나는 종일
종아리를 긁어댔다. 우리는 슬레이트 지붕 위로 무섭게
쏟아지는 빗소리를 들으며 창문 반대편에 걸린 달력 사
진을 바라보는 걸로 지루한 여름을 견뎠다. 투명하고
생생한 햇빛, 푸른 티크나무 숲, 눈 덮인 안나푸르나, 잔

8

When October came, Father hung a *pachhaura* (a rectangular shawl worn by Nepalese men) over the window facing the street. Fog had crept in through the cracks of the crooked framed window during the night, and he had come down with a bad cough. Last summer, the mold under the linoleum spread to the furniture and the clothes hanging on the walls and eventually penetrated Father's lungs and my calves. Father couldn't stop coughing while I couldn't stop scratching. We endured that long summer listening to the rain crashing down onto the slate roof and looking at the calendar pictures on the wall opposite the window. The clear, vivid

9

잔하게 물결치는 페와 호, 그리고 사탕수수를 빨아 먹으며 웃고 있는 아이들…….

아버지와 나는 십여 년 전까지 돼지축사로 쓰였다는, 낡은 베니어판 문 다섯 개가 나란히 붙어 있는 건물에서 살고 있다. 쪽마루도 없는데다 처마마저 참새 꼬리처럼 짧아 아침이면 이슬에 젖은 신발을 신고 학교에 가야 한다. 며칠 전 주인아주머니는 누런 갱지에 '빈 방 있음'이라고 써 3호실 문짝에 붙여놓았다. 그 방 앞을 지나던 나는 열린 문틈으로 안을 들여다보았다. 벽에는 얼룩과 곰팡이와 낙서가 가득했고, 들뜬 황갈색 비닐 장판 위로는 뽀얀 먼지가 살얼음처럼 깔려 있었다. 비스듬하게 세워진 낡은 캐비닛 뒤쪽 벽에는 쥐가 들락거릴 정도의 작고 새까만 구멍이 뚫려 있는데, 구멍 주위로 자잘한 시멘트 가루와 흙덩이가 흩어져 있어 마치 상처 부위에 엉겨 붙은 피딱지처럼 보였다. 총알에 맞아 쿨럭쿨럭 피를 쏟아내는 심장을 본 것 같은 섬뜩함이 가슴을 오그라뜨렸다.

그 방에 살던 파키스탄 청년 알리는 도둑질을 하고 마을을 떠났다. 강풍이 불던 날 밤의 어둠과 소란을 틈타 한방을 쓰던 비재 아저씨의 돈을 훔쳐 달아난 것이

sunlight, the green teak forest, the snow-laden Annapurna ranges, the serene ripples on Phewa Lake, and happy children sucking on sugar canes.

Five worn veneer doors line the outside of our building, which used to be a pig shed up until about ten years ago. Our room is so small we leave our shoes outside. The roof overhang is short like a sparrow's tail and my shoes are wet with dew when I wear them to school in the morning. A few days ago, the landlady taped a yellowed sheet of newsprint to the door of Room 3 on which she had written "Room for Rent." As I passed by one morning, I stopped to take a peek through the slightly cracked open door. The walls were mottled with stains, mold, and scribbles while white dust blanketed the tan linoleum like thin ice. On the wall behind the old leaning cabinet was a small black hole, just the right size for a mouse. In front of the hole were tiny mounds of cement powder and dirt, reminding me of crusty scabs atop a wound. I shuddered as if I had just seen a bullet pierce a human heart and saw the blood gushing out.

Ali, the Pakistani teenager who used to live in that room, had run off with his roommate's money. A fierce wind was blowing the night he decided to

다. 비재 아저씨는 송금 비용을 아끼려고 벽에 구멍을 파서 돈을 숨겨놓았다고 한다. 그날 밤 알리가 돈을 꺼낼 때 나던 조심스런 부스럭거림을 아저씨는 왜 듣지 못했을까. 하긴, 이틀 연속 철야근무에 특근까지 했으니 그럴 만도 하다. 게다가 그날따라 2호실 방글라데시 아주머니의 갓난아기는 밤새 잠을 자지 않고 보챘고, 저녁 내내 텔레비전 앞에서 시끄럽게 떠들던 1호실 미얀마 아저씨들은 나중엔 취한 목소리로 노래를 불러대기까지 했다. 밤에 일하는 5호실의 러시아 아가씨 마리나는 아예 집에 들어오지도 않았다. 4호실에서 사는 아버지와 나만이 일찌감치 불을 끄고 어둠 속에 누워 있었다. 하지만 우리들 역시 머릿속으로는 매우 혼란스러운 생각, 집 나간 어머니 생각에 빠져 있어서 누군가 돈을 훔치느라 바스락대는 소리를 들을 수 없었다.

사실 알리는 비재 아저씨 아들의 생명을 훔쳐 도망간 거나 다름없다. 아저씨는 막내아들의 심장수술 비용을 마련하려고 여기 왔으니까. 이 마을에선 불행이 너무나 흔해 발에 차일 지경이다. 그래서 웬만한 일에는 누구도 신경 쓰지 않는다. 하지만 비재 아저씨가 그날 새벽에 내지른, 절망과 분노에 찬 비명 소리는 한동안 잊히

steal from Mr. Vijay; the turbulence and darkness worked in his favor. Mr. Vijay had been hiding his savings in a hole he had dug in the wall to save on international transfer fees. How could he not hear Ali rustling about the room that night? Well, he had worked two days straight on overtime and night-shifts. On top of that, the Bangladeshi baby in Room 2 was fussy the entire night, and the Burmese men in Room 1 talked loudly while watching TV and then proceeded to belt out songs in their drunkenness. Marina, the Russian girl who worked at night, did not come back to Room 5 until the morning. Father and I, in Room 4, were the first to cut our lights early. We laid there in the darkness. Our minds were both locked in such deep thought, still trying to process Mother leaving us, that we, too, could not hear the rustling noises of the thief.

That night, Ali pretty much ran away with the life of Mr. Vijay's youngest son. Mr. Vijay had found work here to pay for his heart surgery. There are so many misfortunes in this town, you could trip over them in the street. That's why people don't care much. But the furious cry of despair Mr. Vijay let out that dawn will probably not be forgotten for a long time. These days, you can find Mr. Vijay sit-

지 않을 것 같다. 요즈음 아저씨는 마당에 있는 늙은 감나무 밑에 앉아 먼 산을 바라보곤 한다. 어쩌다 산 정상에 구름이 걸리면 저기 물소가 지나간다, 라는 엉뚱한 혼잣말을 하면서. 아무래도 아저씨는 꽤 오래 눈물과 한숨으로 시간을 보내야 할 것 같다. 감나무 꼭대기에 매달린 까치밥이 붉은 속을 뚝뚝 떨어뜨려야 겨울을 날 수 있는 것처럼.

너무 다양한 삶을 보아버린 열세 살 내 머릿속은 히말라야처럼 굴곡이 패어 있다. 세계지도 속의 히말라야는 사실 손가락 한 마디 크기다. 하지만 히말라야는 지도로 그릴 수 없는 땅이라고 아버지는 말했다. 깊게 주름진 계곡과 높은 설산은 세상 전체를 한 바퀴 도는 것보다 더 길 거라면서. 학교 과학실에서 본 뇌 모형을 떠올리니 쉽게 이해가 갔다. 사람도 어려서 다양한 경험을 하면 뇌가 심하게 주름진다니까 내 나이도 빠르게 늘어나고 있을 거다.

3호실이 빠지는 대로 비재 아저씨는 우리 방으로 오기로 했다. 방세를 아낄 수 있어서다. 아버지는 더는 집 나간 어머니를 기다리지 않기로 결심한 걸까. 하긴 어머니는 조선족이니까 어디서든 살아갈 수 있다. 적어도

14

ting under the aged persimmon tree in the yard as he gazes at the mountains in the distance. He mutters nonsense once in a while, referring to the cloud clinging to the mountaintop as a water buffalo, for example. It looks like he will have to spend quite some time in tears and deep sighs before he recovers. It's like waiting for the spring. Winter isn't over until the last of the persimmons left for the magpies on the uppermost branches let go of their red overripe insides.

The winding bends of my thirteen-year-old mind are riddled like the Himalayas by the range of lifestyles I've become privy to. On the world map, the Himalayan range is only as big as your fingertip. But Father said the Himalayas could never be accurately represented on a map because the combined distance between the deep, furrowed valleys and the high, snow-laden mountain peaks would be great enough to circle the Earth more than once. Picturing the brain model I saw in the school science lab helped me understand what he meant. Since deep folds start forming in your brain when you're exposed to a variety of experiences at a young age, my brain is most likely very old.

Mr. Vijay decided to move in with us as soon as

자신에게 수치를 주거나 학대하려 드는 사람들에게 한국말로 대꾸할 수는 있을 테지. 그만 때리세요, 왜 욕해요, 돈 주세요 따위 말고도 여러 가지 어려운 말들을. 선처, 멸시, 응급실, 피해 보상, 심지어 밑구멍으로 호박씨 깐다느니, 개 발에 땀난다는 말까지.

잠에서 깨어나니, 로티(밀가루 빵) 굽는 냄새가 방 안 가득하다. 방문 쪽으로 돌아앉아 밀가루 반죽을 방망이로 밀어대는 아버지의 등과 어깨는 물결처럼 출렁인다. 내 발치께 버너 위에 올려진 주전자에선 버터차 치아가 쉐쉐 가쁜 숨소리를 낸다.

그러고 보니 오늘이 아버지의 마흔 번째 생일이다. 좀 전까지 몰랐는데 달력에 동그라미가 쳐진 걸 보니 분명히 그렇다. 해마다 가을이면 아버지는 티알 축제(한국의 추석 같은 다사잉 명절 15일 뒤에 오는 네팔의 축제)를 마치고 생일날 아침에 고향을 떠나온 이야기를 입버릇처럼 되풀이했다. "네팔의 여름 햇빛은 정수리로 내려오고 가을 햇빛은 가슴에 와 닿지. 내가 그곳을 떠난 건 성긴 햇살이 비스듬히 내려와 심장에 꽂히는 가을이었단다. 심장이 사납게 뛰는 스물여섯……." 어쩌자고 동그라미를 그토록 크게 그려넣었는지 모르겠다. 어차피 선물도

16

he could find someone to rent Room 3, which he needed to do to save money on rent, of course. I wonder if Father gave up waiting for Mother. She *is Chosunjok* after all; those ethnic Koreans can survive anywhere. If anyone tried to shame or abuse her, she'd be able to snap back in Korean at least. Stop hitting me. Must you swear? Please give me some money. She even knew hard words like benevolence, disdain, emergency room and damage compensation, as well as expressions like, "hulling pumpkin seeds under the table" and "working the dog until his paws sweat."

The next morning, I wake up to the scent of fresh *roti* (flatbread made with flour). Father is rolling out the dough with a wooden rod. His back and shoulders sway like the waves. A kettle of *chiya* butter tea whistles and wheezes on the gas burner by my feet.

I realize that it's Father's fortieth birthday today. I had forgotten about it until I saw today's date circled on the calendar. Every year, when autumn comes, Father recounts the story of how he left his homeland. It was the morning of his birthday; the Tihar festival had just ended. Tihar is the second largest festival in Nepal, held 15 days after Dashain,

못할 텐데. 아버지는 어린아이인 나한테까지 용돈을 줄 여유가 없다.

검은 색연필로 여러 번 덧그린 커다란 원은 마치 '외' 처럼 보인다. '외'는 미얀마 말로 '소용돌이'란 뜻이다. 1 호실 미얀마 아저씨들은, 한국에 온 외국인 노동자들은 모두 '외'에 빠진 거라고 말한다. 나는 아버지의 소용돌 이 삶 속에서 태어났으니 새끼 외다. 하지만 한국에서, 조선족 어머니 자궁에서 태어났으니 반쪽 외다. 물론 그렇다고 해서 내가 학교나 마을에서 외 취급을 받지 않을 거란 착각을 할 정도의 머저리는 아니다. 자리에 누운 채 왼뺨의 광대뼈 부위를 만져본다. 조금 부었는 지 손바닥에 그득하게 잡힌다. "너 소영이 짝이지? 이 더러운 자식!" 어제 오후 집으로 돌아오는데 6학년 소영 이 오빠가 다짜고짜 내 멱살을 잡았다. 그러고는 똥 닦 는 냄새 나는 손으로 왜 소영이를 만졌느냐고 다그쳤 다. 난 그런 적 없다고 했다. 연필이 굴러가서 잡으려다 가 실수로 손등을 건드린 거라고 구차한 기분이 들 정 도로 차근차근 설명했다. 소영이 오빠는 거짓말 마 새 꺄, 라며 주먹을 날렸다. 나도 녀석의 옆구리를 한 대 갈 겨주었다. 쓰러진 녀석의 코에서 피가 나와 옷이 피투

equivalent to Korean *Chuseok.* "In Nepal, the summer sunlight rests on the crown of your head. The autumn sunlight touches your heart. I left Nepal in the autumn, when the sparse sunlight came down at a slant and penetrated my heart. I was twenty-six years old, heart still racing hard." Why he had drawn such a big circle I don't know. He knew there wouldn't be any presents. He didn't even have the luxury to give a little kid like me some allowance.

He had drawn the large circle with a black colored pencil and traced over it several times. It looked like the Burmese word *oue,* meaning whirlpool. The Burmese men in Room 1 say that all migrant workers who come to Korea are caught in a *oue*. Being born out of my father's whirlpool life would make me baby *oue* status. But the fact that I came from a *Chosunjok* womb makes me only half *oue*. Needless to say, I know I'll still be treated like a *oue* at school or in town. I'm not that stupid. As I lay there, I feel my left cheekbone. It must've been pretty swollen; it was firm to the touch.

"You're the guy who sits next to So-yeong, aren't you? You dirty bastard!" Out of the blue, So-yeong's older brother in the sixth grade had grabbed me

성이가 되었다.

"손으로 먹어라. 그래야 서둘러 먹지 않고 과식하지 않는단다."

아버지 말을 못 들은 체하고 나는 젓가락으로 로티를 찢는다. 과식할 음식이나 있냐고 반박하려다 참는다. 늬들은 손으로 밥 먹고 손으로 밑 닦는다면서? 우엑, 더러워. 놀려대는 반 아이들 목소리가 들리는 듯하다. 그건 사실이 아니다. 밥은 밑 닦는 왼손이 아닌 오른손으로 먹는다. 그 때문에 아버지는 언제나 오른손을 깨끗하게, 귀하게 다룬다. 다만 아버지 손가락에는 등고선처럼 생긴 지문이 없다. 닳아버린 지 오래여서 지장을 찍으면 짓이겨진 꽃물자국 같은 게 묻어난다. 사람들은 지문이 없으니 영혼도 없다고 생각하나 보다. 그렇지 않다면 노끈에 꿰인 가자미처럼 취급당할 리가 없다. 야 임마, 혹은 씨발놈아, 라는 이름의 외국인 노동자 한 꿰미. 말린고꽃을 좋아하고 민요 〈러섬피리리〉를 구성지게 부르는, 안나푸르나의 추억을 가진 '어루준'이란 이름의 사람은 처음부터 있지도 않다.

"멍이 들었구나. 어쩌다 그런 거냐?"

오른손으로 로티를 찢어 입에 넣으면서 묻는 아버지

by the neck on my way home from school yesterday afternoon.

"How dare you touch my little sister with the
same filthy hand you use to wipe your ass?"

"I didn't." I explained that my pencil had started
rolling away and that when I tried to stop it, my
hand brushed against the back of hers. It was pa-
thetic having to give such a detailed play-by-play
of the incident.

So-yeong's brother threw a punch at me, calling
me a lying bastard. I swung at his side so hard he
fell to the ground. Blood trickled from his nose and
dripped onto his shirt.

"Eat with your hands. That way, you won't rush or
overeat."

Pretending not to have heard Father speak, I tear
the *roti* with my chopsticks. I want to snap back, "I
couldn't overeat even if I wanted to." I can hear the
voices of my classmates teasing me. "So, I hear you
guys eat with your hands and wipe with them too?"
"Ew. That's gross."

But they have it wrong. The right hand is used
for eating and the left for wiping. That's why Father
took special care to keep his right hand clean at all
times. Father's hands were so worn that there were

한테 나는 사실대로 말했다.

"사실이란 중요하지 않아. 아무도 우리 말을 믿어주지 않으니까."

부정확한 발음으로 한국말을 떠듬거리는 아버지는 어릿광대를 연상시킨다. 말이 어눌하면 누구나 멍청하게 보이는 법이다.

"차라리 맞았다면 나았을 텐데……. 조심해라. 그 애가 가만있진 않을 거야."

"저도 자신 있어요."

"바보 같은 소리 마. 다음에라도 녀석이 때리거든 피하지 말고 맞아줘."

아버지는 갑자기 네팔 말로 말한다. 내 눈을 똑바로 바라보더니 이번엔 턱에 힘을 주며 말도 안 되는 네팔 속담을 들이댄다.

"누군가 돌을 던지거든 꽃을 던져주라고 했다."

"싫어요, 난. 차라리 사람들을 갈겨버리고 말지. 이담에 팔뚝에 힘이 붙으면 절대 아버지처럼 공장 일이나 하진 않을 거야. 우리를 업신여기고 괴롭히는 나쁜 놈들을 때려눕히고 발로 차고……."

"야크처럼 앞뒤 재지 않고 돌진하겠다는 거냐?"

no more ridges to his fingerprints, like a map without any contour lines. On official papers, his thumbprint looked like a crushed flower petal. People must have thought that you had no soul if you had no fingerprints. I mean, why else would they have treated Father like a string of flatfish hung up to dry? A lifeless migrant worker answering to "Hey, you" and "Asshole." A person going by the name of Arjun—who likes *malingo* flowers and can sing a mean "Resham Phiriri," who has fond memories of the Annapurna range—never existed from the beginning.

"You've got yourself a pretty bad bruise," my father studies the rise of my left cheek. "What happened?"

I recount the story as he tears off a piece of *roti* with his right hand and puts it in his mouth.

"The facts don't matter. Nobody believes what we say, anyway."

His poor Korean pronunciation and stammering make him sound like a clown when he speaks in Korean. That's because anyone who can't speak properly looks dumb.

"You shouldn't have fought back... Be careful. He's probably not done with you yet."

"야크가 어떻게 뛰는지 알 게 뭐예요. 히말라야 얘기라면 이제 지긋지긋해요."

반사적으로 튀어나온 말에 나도 놀라고 만다. 하지만 참았던 말들은 멈추지 않고 계속 쏟아져나온다.

"난 여기, 식사동 가구공단밖에 몰라요. 흐리멍덩한 하늘이랑 깨진 벽돌 더미, 그리고 냄새 나는 바람. 나한텐 이게 전부죠. 게다가 집 나간 바람둥이 엄마까지……."

"입 닥치지 못해!"

뺨이 얼얼하다. 아버지는 거친 숨을 내쉬며 주먹을 쥔 채 부르르 떤다. 볼을 싸쥐고 방에서 뛰쳐나오니 마당에 있던 누군가 나마스테('안녕하세요'라는 뜻의 네팔 인사말), 하고 인사를 건넨다. 나는 대꾸하지 않고 이슬에 젖은 신발을 꿰어 마당을 가로지른다. 수돗가에 떨어져 있던 감 하나가 발밑에서 터져 으깨진다.

뱃속에서 울리는 끄르륵 소리를 들으며 나는 공장이 늘어선 골목으로 들어선다. 메마르고 갈라진 시멘트 길, 칙칙한 작업복 차림의 사람들, 공장 지붕 위로 떨어지는 희뿌연 햇빛, 그리고 이따금 사나운 짐승처럼 달

"I can take him."

"That's foolish thinking. The next time he tries to hit you, let him."

Father suddenly switches to Nepalese. Looking me square in the eyes, he sets his jaws and repeats a ridiculous Nepali saying.

"*Kasaile timilai dhunga hanchha bhane timi uslai fulle hanidi nu.*" It means, "If someone throws you a stone, throw him a flower."

"No way. I'd knock him down. When I get older and grow some muscle on these arms, you're not going to find me at a factory like you, Father. All those jerks that look down on us and harass us—I'm gonna slam them to the ground and kick their lights out..."

"So you're going to charge at them blindly like a yak would?"

"I don't care about yaks. I'm sick of hearing about the Himalayas."

I surprise myself at the words that shot out of my own mouth. But the feelings that had been pent up inside of me insist on making themselves known.

"This place—Siksa-dong furniture complex—is the only place I know. The hazy sky, the heaps of broken brick, the foul air. That's it. Oh, and the

려가는 짐 실은 트럭들 사이에서 현기증을 느낀다. 오늘처럼 학교에서 급식을 하지 않는 토요일엔 늘 이렇다. 아침에 먹은 치아 한 잔으로는 오후까지 견디기가 쉽지 않다. 공장에서 나오는 시끄러운 소음, 페인트 냄새, 가구공장의 옻 냄새가 빈속을 메스껍게 한다. 코를 움켜쥔 채 인력 구함, 사채 쓸 분, 빅토리아 관광나이트 따위의 광고지가 덕지덕지 붙은 더러운 공장 벽과 전봇대를 지난다. 염색공장에서 나오는 새빨간 물이 도랑을 붉게 물들이며 흘러간다. 김이 모락모락 나는 게 갓 잡은 돼지 피처럼 보인다. 헛구역질이 난다. 입 안에서 씁쓰름한 위액이 느껴진다. 내가 죽게 된다면 아마 코부터 썩을 거다. 태어나서 지금껏 냄새 속에 살았으니까. 독한 화학약품 냄새들은 실핏줄을 타고 머릿속까지 들어가 언젠가 나를 멍청하게 만들 테지. 어차피 상관없다. 머리를 굴리면 굴릴수록 세상 살기 힘들다니까. 언젠가 아버지는 말했다. "머리를 굴려 이 지옥에 떨어졌어. 다른 청년들처럼 산에서 염소를 기르거나 들에서 농사일을 했더라면, 강물에 몸을 씻고 집으로 돌아와 구수한 달(콩 수프), 바트(밥) 냄새를 맡으며 신께 감사할 줄 알았다면……." 미래슈퍼 앞에 다다르자 출입문에

mom that cheated on us."

"Shut your mouth!"

My cheek stings. Father breathes heavily, his hand still clenched in a tight fist, his body trembling. I cup my cheek and run out of the room. Someone in the yard greets me with "*Namaste,*" but I don't respond. I put on my shoes, dampened by the dew, and cross the yard. A persimmon that had fallen by the communal sinks bursts under my shoe.

My stomach growls as I turn the bend into the street lined with the factories. The parched and cracked cement road. The factory workers in their drab uniforms. The hazy sunlight above the factory rooftops. Loaded trucks storming by like fierce beasts once every so often. I start feeling light-headed. It's like this every Saturday—when there's no school lunch.

The cup of *chiya* tea I had in the morning has to sustain me until dinner, and it's not easy. The noise and the mixed smells of paint and clothes from the factory make my empty stomach churn. I plug my nose and walk past the dirty factory walls and utility poles, both plastered with ads for hiring, private

27

붙어 있는 오렌지 빛 음료수 '쿠우' 광고가 눈에 들어온다. 입 안에 침이 돌면서 울렁거림이 가라앉는다. 바지 주머니를 흔들자 짤랑거리는 소리가 난다. 손을 넣어 꺼내보니 종잇조각 몇 개와 구슬, 병뚜껑, 녹슨 못, 그리고 먼지가 나온다.

멀리 알루미늄공장 쪽에서 누군가 걸어오고 있다. 자세히 보니 쿤 형이다. 사 년 전에 한국에 들어온 그는 나보다 열두 살이 위인 스물다섯이다. 그가 처음 마을에 왔을 때가 생각난다. 까만 배낭을 메고 방을 얻으러 다니던 쿤은 아버지를 만나자, 아니 아버지 입에서 계곡물에 자갈 굴러가는 듯한 네팔 말이 흘러나오자 갑자기 눈물을 줄줄 흘렸다. 아버지는 그가 몹시 힘들게 지냈다는 걸 금방 알아차렸다. 그의 얼굴 표정에서 산업연수생 시절에 겪었던 어려움이 그대로 드러났다. 지하방에서 휴일도 없이 하루 열여섯 시간씩 일하다가 한밤중에 창문으로 도망쳤다는 그의 몸은 시퍼런 멍과 상처로 얼룩져 있었고 화덕처럼 뜨거웠다. 아버지는 네팔의 민간요법인 쌀소주를 만들어주었다. 달구어진 팬에 기름을 치고 생쌀을 넣어 튀긴 다음 소주를 붓고 한동안 뚜껑을 닫아놓았다가 따끈해진 액체를 소주잔에 따랐다.

loans, and the Victoria Nightclub. The crimson water from the dye-works factory reddens the ditchwater as it swirls its way by. The ballooning steam from the smokestacks reminds me of blood gushing from a freshly slaughtered pig. I gag at the thought. I can taste the bitter gastric juices in my mouth. When I die, my nose will probably be the first thing to rot. I've been inhaling stenches from the day I was born, that's why. I'm sure the smell of toxic chemicals traveling through my capillary veins to my brain will make me stupid someday. It doesn't matter, anyways.

They say that the more you use your head, the harder it is to live in this world. Father once said, "I used my head and landed in this hell of a place. If only I stayed to raise goats on the mountain or farm in the fields like the other young men... If only I had known to be thankful to the gods for being able to come home to the smell of creamy *dahl baht* (lentil soup and rice) after washing in the river..." I reach Mirae Supermarket and spot an ad for the orange Qoo drink on the door. My mouth waters and my churning stomach settles. I tap my pockets and hear clinking. I reach in and pull out some paper scraps, a marble, a bottle cap, a rusty nail, and

연거푸 석 잔을 마시게 했더니 열에 들떠 있던 쿤은 금방 잠들었다. 다음 날 아침에 쿤의 몸은 많이 회복되었다. 크게 쌍꺼풀진 눈에는 전날의 공포와 우울 대신, 숨어 있던 촌스러움이 드러났다. 돈을 벌어 귀국하겠다는, 한 달에 오십만 원을 벌어 반쯤 저축하겠다는, 딱 삼 년만 참으면 된다는 순진한 믿음 같은.

쿤은 지금 리바이스 청바지에 나이키 점퍼를 입고 있다. 동대문시장에서 산 짝퉁이지만 제법 그럴듯해 보인다. 그는 이목구비가 뚜렷하고 피부가 흰 아르레족(네팔의 여러 부족 중 하나로 아리안계에 속함)이라 머리를 노랗게 염색하니 얼핏 미국 사람처럼 보인다. 하긴 일부러 그렇게 보이려고 염색을 했을 테지만. 언젠가 명동에 다녀온 그가 입술을 비틀며 말했다. "한국 사람들은 단일민족이라 외국인한테 거부감을 갖는다고? 그래서 이주 노동자들한테 불친절한 거라고? 웃기는 소리 마. 미국 사람 앞에서는 안 그래. 친절하다 못해 비굴할 정도지. 너도 얼굴만 좀 하얗다면 미국 사람처럼 보일 텐데……."

그 뒤로 나는 저녁마다 물에 탈색제 한 알을 풀어 세수했고 저녁이면 내가 얼마나 하얘졌나 보려고 거울 앞

some lint.

Someone is walking my way from the distant aluminum factory. I look carefully. It's Khun. He came to Korea four years ago and is twenty-five years old, twelve years older than me. I remember when Father first brought him home. Wearing a black backpack, Khun was out looking for a room to rent when he met Father. The moment he heard Father speak Nepali—the sound of pebbles being pushed up against the shore—tears streamed down his face. Instantly, Father saw how hard it must have been for Khun. His face told the story of his rough days as an industrial trainee. He had been working sixteen-hour days in a basement without rest when he decided to escape through a window in the middle of the night. When he came to our house, his body was cut, bruised, and burning up. Father made rice *soju*, a Nepali household remedy for bringing down fevers. After frying raw rice in a hot, oiled pan, he added some *soju* and let it simmer with the lid on. He then poured the hot alcohol into a shot glass. He had Khun drink three glasses in a row, and he fell asleep soon after. The next morning, Khun was much improved. Instead of fear and gloom, his big eyes now revealed a hidden

으로 달려갔다. 푸른 새벽 공기 속에서 하얗게 각질이 일어난 내 얼굴을 볼 때면 가슴이 설레었다. 내가 바라는 건 미국 사람처럼 되는 게 아니었다. 그냥 한국 사람만큼만 하얗게, 아니 노랗게 되기를 바랐다. 여름 숲의 뱀처럼, 가을 낙엽 밑의 나방처럼 나에게도 보호색이 필요했다. 남의 눈에 띄지 않고 조용히 살아갈 수 있도록. 비비총을 새로 산 남자애들의 첫 번째 표적이 되지 않고, 적이 필요한 아이들의 왕따가 되지 않고, 달리기를 할 때 뒤에서 밀치고 싶은 까만 방해물로 비치지 않도록. 나는 하루도 거르지 않고 탈색제를 썼다. 그러던 어느 날, 세수를 하고 있는데 누군가 내 세숫대야의 물을 거칠게 쏟아버렸다. 고개를 들어보니 아버지였다. 아버지는 탈색제가 든 비닐봉지를 수돗가에 내동댕이쳤다. 나는 뒷덜미를 잡힌 채 방으로 질질 끌려들어가 멍이 시퍼렇게 들도록 종아리를 맞았다. 그날 밤, 오랜만에 술 냄새를 풍기며 자정이 다 되어 들어온 아버지는 주머니에서 '누크' 베이비로션을 꺼냈다. 그러고는 붉은 실핏줄이 보일 만큼 껍질이 벗겨진 내 얼굴에 로션을 잔뜩 발라주었다. 투박하고 거친 손바닥으로 뺨을 아프도록 쓰다듬으면서. 그러고 나서 아버지는 이불을

rustic charm. The kind of naïve confidence that led him to dream he would earn money and return home, that he would make five hundred thousand *won* a month and save half, that he would be able to leave after three years.

Khun is wearing Levis jeans and a Nike jacket. I know they are imitations bought for cheap at Dongdaemun Market, but you can barely tell. He has defined facial features, and his hair is dyed blonde. He was a fair-skinned *Arere*, one of the Nepali tribes of Aryan descent, and could almost pass for an American. That's probably why he dyed his hair in the first place. I remember what he told me upon returning from a trip to Myeongdong. "Don't be fooled. Koreans may say they're uncomfortable with foreigners because they're a homogenous nation, and that that's why migrant workers are treated the way they are. Shoot, they're not like that to Americans," he sneered. "Polite doesn't cut it. Koreans would get on their hands and knees for Americans. If your face was a bit whiter, you'd look American..."

From that day forward, I started to add a little bit of bleach into the water I used to wash my face at night. After washing, I'd run inside to see how pale

머리끝까지 뒤집어쓰더니 잠들기 직전까지 흐느꼈다. 가끔 뜻을 알 수 없는 네팔 말을, 몹시 지친 목소리로 중얼거리며.

쿤이 작업복 점퍼 안쪽 주머니에 손을 넣고 걸어온다. 가슴께가 불룩하게 튀어나온 걸 보니 뭔가 맛있는 거라도 숨기고 있는 게 분명하다. 그에게 달려가 숨긴 걸 달라고 졸라댄다. 쿤은 얼굴을 찡그린다. 쿤의 옆구리에 손가락을 넣고 꼬물거린다. 간지럼을 잘 타는 쿤은 흐으, 흐으, 김빠진 웃음을 내뱉더니 할 수 없이 그 비밀을 펼쳐 보인다. 흰 붕대에 감긴 손이 허공으로 불쑥 솟아오른다.

"왜 이래?"

"어제 일하다가 그만……. 다행히 손가락 세 개는 남았어."

쿤은 아무렇지도 않다는 듯이 말하려고 애쓴다. 하지만 결국 알아들을 수 없는 말을 내뱉는다. 박치니가(씨발)! 그는 발끝으로 돌멩이를 세게 걷어찬다. 찰랑, 흩날리는 노란 머리카락 사이로 새로 돋는 까만 머리카락이 보인다. 그는 이제 더는 염색을 하지 않을 거다. 여기까지 와서 프레스에 손가락을 잘리는 미국 사람은 없을

I got. In the crisp, early morning, I'd look in the mirror again and see a few dry white flakes on my face. That was exciting. I wasn't trying to look like a completely white person. Just pale enough—no, yellow enough like a Korean person. I needed protective coloring; like a snake in the summer forest, a moth on an autumn leaf. That way, I'd be able to blend in and live a quiet life. That way, I wouldn't be the go-to target of the boys with new BB guns or the outcast for bullies to pick on or the dark-skinned obstruction that kids push out of the way during recess. I used the bleach daily, not skipping a single day.

Then one day, I was washing my face when the entire basin of water was upturned from under me. I looked up and saw it was Father. He took the plastic bag of bleach and hurled it at the spigots. He dragged me by the back of my neck into the room and spanked me until my calves bruised. He came home close to midnight that night, smelling like alcohol for the first time in a long time. From his pocket he pulled out a bottle of NUK baby lotion and proceeded to smear it on my face. The bleach had stripped my face, exposing the red veins underneath. He rubbed the lotion onto my

테니.

"형, 그 손가락 나 주라."

쿤은 멍한 얼굴로 나를 쳐다본다.

"왜?"

"그냥……. 응? 나 주라."

휴지로 돌돌 만 뭉치를 내 손바닥 위에 올려놓는다. 길 양편에 늘어선 전깃줄이 바람에 징징 울어댄다. 바랜 햇빛과 회색 먼지 속을 걷는 쿤의 뒷모습이 늙고 지쳐 보인다.

2호실 아기가 칭얼대는 소리만 들릴 뿐 축사 건물 전체가 조용하다. 나는 마당 한쪽에 있는 감나무 밑으로 다가간다. 커다란 돌멩이를 들추니 까맣고 축축한 흙이 드러난다. 삭정이를 주워 와 땅을 파헤친다. 굵다란 지렁이 한 마리가 햇빛에 놀라 꿈틀대더니 이내 흙 속으로 파고든다. 좀 더 깊이 파헤쳐보지만 개미 새끼 몇 마리뿐 아무것도 눈에 띄지 않는다. 벌써 다 썩어버렸나? 돈을 훔쳐 달아난 알리의 손가락을 초여름에 다섯 개나 묻었는데 하나도 없다. 작년에 묻은 베트남 아저씨 손가락은 말할 것도 없고. 좀 더 깊이 땅을 파려고 팔에 힘

cheeks with his rough, coarse fingers until it hurt. When he finished, he lay down, pulled the blanket over his head and sobbed himself to sleep. He muttered in between the sobs, sometimes in Nepali words I couldn't understand. He sounded extremely tired.

Khun comes walking with one hand inside the inner pocket of his work jacket. His chest is bulging and I'm sure he's hiding food in there. I race to him and beg to see what he's hiding. He scowls. Knowing that he's ticklish, I start poking at his side. After letting out a few lifeless laughs, he gives up and exposes his secret. Out into the air comes a heavily bandaged hand.

"What happened?"

"Yesterday, at work... Luckily, I still have three fingers."

Khun tries to play it off as if it wasn't a big deal. But then he lets out a word I don't understand. *"Bakchiniga!"* Fuck!

He kicks a stone. Dark roots have started to grow out underneath his free-flowing blonde locks. There's no need to dye his hair anymore. No one's going to believe that an American came to Korea to have his fingers cut off in a press.

을 준다. 흙덩이가 부서지면서 얼굴에 튄다. 그러고 보면 알리도 대단하다. 돈을 훔칠 때 어떻게 한쪽 손만으로 캐비닛을 밀치고, 벽을 파헤칠 수 있었을까. 삭정이가 툭, 부러진다. 순간 하얀 뼈다귀들이 무더기로 쏟아져 나온다. 그러면 그렇지. 나는 주머니에서 손가락을 꺼낸다. 휴지에 말렸던 검붉은 손가락을 뼈다귀들 틈에 놓는다. 물든 감잎 하나가 손가락 위로 살며시 내려앉는다. 나는 구덩이에 흙을 푹, 밀어넣는다. 수돗가 쪽으로 침을 퉤 뱉고 나서 두 손을 모은다. '파괴의 신 시바님, 이 정도면 충분해요. 더는 제물을 바라지 마세요. 특히 아버지하고 제 손가락만큼은 절대.'

맹꽁이 자물통에 열쇠를 끼워 비틀고 문을 여니 방안이 엉망이다. 냄비에는 어제 먹다 남긴 라면 부스러기가 퉁퉁 불어 애벌레처럼 떠 있고 발길에 차여 넘어진 찻잔에선 치아가 흘러나와 콧물처럼 말라간다. 둘둘 말아 창문 아래 밀어놓은 이불 위에는 벗어놓은 옷가지가 흩어져 있다. 가방을 구석에 내동댕이치고 옷더미 위로 풀썩 드러눕는다.

"안녕?" 창문에 매달린 코끼리는 여전히 말이 없다. 무심한 눈길로 먼 곳을 쳐다볼 뿐. 일곱 개의 코를 가진,

"Hey, Khun, can I have those fingers?" I ask.

He gives me a blank stare.

"Why?"

"Just 'cuz. Please? Let me have them?"

He places a small bundle of tissue in my hand. The electric wires lining both sides of the street whine in the wind. I watch Khun walk away through the faded sunlight and gray dust. He looks old and weary from behind.

Other than the fussy baby in Room 2, the rest of the building that once housed livestock is quiet. I walk toward the persimmon tree in the side of the yard and step under it. I overturn a big rock to find dark, moist soil. I find a dead branch nearby and start digging. A fat earthworm squirms upon seeing the sunlight and wriggles its way back into the dirt. I dig deeper but don't see anything but a few ants. Did they rot already?

Earlier that summer, I had buried five of Ali's fingers there—the guy who fled with the money. There was also the Vietnamese guy's finger from last year. I decide to try digging a bit deeper and take a whack at the hole. Dirt sprays my face as I strike a hardened clump. If you think about it, Ali's

퍼체우라에 은사로 화려하게 수놓인 그 코끼리는 원래 신들의 왕 인드라를 태우는 구름이었다고 한다. "그래서요?" 창문에 퍼체우라를 달다가 그 이야기를 들은 나는 흥분해서 아버지를 재촉했다. "어느 날 창조주 브라마가 '세계의 알'을 깨뜨리면서 코끼리의 격이 낮아져 그만 우주를 떠받치는 기둥이 되었단다." 나는 눈을 질끈 감았다. 아버지는 슬쩍 내 안색을 살폈다. "어차피 그건 힌두교 신화일 뿐이야. 신이 깨뜨린 알이란 없어." 순간 못대가리에서 미끄러져 엇나간 망치가 아버지 손톱을 찧었다. 손톱 끝에 침을 바르고 통증을 참던 아버지는 떨어진 못을 찾으려고 두 손을 뻗어 바닥을 더듬었다. 문득 아버지가 코끼리처럼 여겨졌다. 구름보다 높은 히말라야에서 태어나 이곳, 후미진 공장지대에서 살아가고 있으니…….

어디선가 노랫소리가 들려온다. 가늘게 떨리는 그 목소리 주인은 2호실 토야 엄마다. 모레니에 절로 세이데세, 모레니에 절로 세이데세, 날 그곳으로 데려다주세요, 날 그곳으로 데려다주세요……. 지난봄에 단속반을 피해 뒷산으로 도망치다가 발목을 삐어 결국 잡히고 만 토야 아빠는 스리랑카로 추방된 뒤 돌아오지 못하고 있

getaway was quite impressive. I mean, he was able to push the cabinet aside and dig out the money from the wall with just one hand. The branch snaps. Then, I see the pile of white bones. I knew I had the right spot. I take out the bundle in my pocket. I peel the tissue from the dried, wine-colored fingers and place them on top of the bones. A falling persimmon leaf gently lands on the fingers. I fill the hole with dirt again. I spit on the ground and put my hands together. "Shiva, god of destruction, surely this ought to do. Please don't expect any more offerings from me. Especially not my fingers or Father's."

I stick my key into the padlock, turn it and open the door to a messy room. Leftover pieces of soggy *ramyeon* noodles float like maggots in the pot. A trickle of *chiya* tea from the cup that had been knocked over dries like a runny nose. Clothes are strewn on top of the bedding that was rolled up and pushed beneath the window. I fling my backpack into a corner of the room and sprawl out on the blankets.

"Hi, there." The elephant hanging from the window has yet to reply. The seven-trunked elephant stares indifferently into the distance. Richly em-

다. 혼자 남은 토야 엄마는 집에서 기계부품에 나사를 꿰어 버는 푼돈으로 연명하는 눈치다. 홀둘리아 푸자 토레 게노 펠레라코 헬라거리, 탈 모르넷 아게 슈두 바레크 피레아쇼크, 기도꽃을 꺾어 왜 그냥 버렸을까, 사랑하는 사람 죽기 전에 다시 돌아오세요……. 갑자기 어머니 생각이 난다. 신 김치와 미역국 냄새, 연한 레몬 로션 냄새, 그리고 뭐라고 이름 붙일 수 없지만 스르르 잠이 오게 하는 신비한 살내까지. 지난봄에 어머니가 남기고 간 냄새는 한동안 방 안 어딘가에 남아 미풍이 불 때마다 언뜻언뜻 맡아졌다. 하지만 이제 방 안에선 그 냄새가 나지 않는다. 퀴퀴한 홀아비 냄새와 지독한 곰팡내가 진동할 뿐이다.

환기를 시키려고 퍼체우라를 젖힌다. 노란 햇빛이 반대편 벽에 있는 히말라야 달력 사진에 내려앉아 너울댄다. 투명하고 생생한 햇빛, 푸른 티크나무 숲, 눈 덮인 안나푸르나, 잔잔하게 물결치는 페와 호, 그리고 사탕수수를 빨아 먹으며 환하게 웃는 아이들……. 아버지는 해마다 똑같은 달력을 사 온다. 아버지가 그 사진을 보면서 기쁨을 얻듯이 나도 그렇게 되기를 바라는 걸까? 하지만 내 눈엔 오후 빛을 받은 히말라야가 금으로

broidered onto the *pachhaura* with spun silver, the elephant, I was told, was once a cloud that carried Indra, the king of the gods.

"What happened to him?"

Father had started to tell the story when he hung the *pachhaura* and I wanted to hear more. "One day, the Creator Brahma broke the golden egg and the elephant's status was lowered to that of a pillar bearing the weight of the universe." When I closed my eyes tight, Father quickly glances at me, wondering what I was thinking.

"It's just Hindu mythology, anyway. The golden egg never existed."

At that moment, the hammer slid off the nail head and struck the tip of his finger. Trying not to show pain, Father sucked on his fingertip, got on his hands and knees and felt around the floor for the nail. He reminded me of the elephant all of sudden —born above the Himalayan clouds, but now here in an obscure factory district.

I hear singing from somewhere. The weak, trembling voice belonged to Toya's mom from Room 2. "*Morenie jullo seyidese, Morenie jullo seyidese.*" Take me to that place, take me to that place... Last spring, Toya's dad was deported to Sri Lanka after

씌운 어금니처럼 보일 뿐이다. 햇빛에 녹아내리기 직전의 노란 바닐라 아이스크림이거나. 달력에서는 여전히 검고 굵은 동그라미가 소용돌이치고 있다. 마음이 편치 않다. 요즘엔 이상하게도 입에서 아무 말이나 튀어나온다. 학교에서 내내 긴장하다가 집에 돌아오면 모든 게 귀찮고, 무엇보다 화가 난다. 오늘은 소영이 오빠가 친구들을 데리고 쉬는 시간마다 우리 교실로 내려왔다. 나는 화장실에 숨어 있다가 수업이 시작된 뒤에야 교실로 들어갈 수 있었다. 겁이 나서가 아니었다. 일대일이라면 자신 있었다. 하지만 한꺼번에 덤벼들어 쥐 잡듯 나를 짓밟는다면, 앞으로 나를 볼 때마다 누구든 그 장면을 떠올릴 것이다. 그것만은 정말 견디기 힘들 것 같았다.

아기 손바닥만큼 작아진 빛은 퍼체우라가 흔들릴 때마다 놀란 듯 부르르 떤다. 갑자기 잠이 몰려온다. 아버지처럼 고향 가는 꿈이라도 꿀 수 있다면 좋겠다. 밤마다 아버지는 낡은 춤바를 입고 고향 마을로 찾아가는 꿈을 꾼다. 노란 유채꽃 언덕 너머 보이는 눈부신 설산과 낯익은 황토 집, 정다운 마을 사람들이 있는 곳으로. 꿈에서 아버지는 가녀린 퉁게꽃과 붉은 비저꽃이 흐드

he got caught trying to run away towards the mountains. He was outrunning the squad when he twisted his ankle. He hasn't returned since. Left to fend for herself, Toya's mom gets by with the small sum she makes attaching screws to machine parts at home. *"Huldulia puja tore geno pelelako helagali. Tal morenet agae shudu bareke pireashoke."* Why did you throw my prayers away? Come back before your loved one dies... I'm reminded of Mother all of a sudden. The aroma of well-fermented kimchi and *miyeokguk,* the faint scent of lemon lotion, even the comforting smell of her skin that's hard to put a name to but that puts you to sleep. The smell she left behind last spring lingered for a while. And whenever the slightest wind blew, you could catch whiffs of it. But it has completely left the room now. The musty smell of old men and that awful mold has taken over.

I draw back the *pachhaura* to ventilate the room. The golden sunlight dances on the Himalaya calendar across the room. The clear, vivid sunlight, the green teak forest, the snow-laden Annapurna range, the serene ripples of Phewa Lake, and happy children sucking on sugar canes... Father buys the same calendar every year. I wonder if he hopes

러진 고향집 마당으로 들어서서는 가족과 친지에 둘러싸여 달과 바트, 더르가리(야채 반찬), 물소고기에 토마토 양념을 발라 구운 첼라를 실컷 먹는다고 했다. 하지만 다음날 공항에서 비행기에 오르려고 하면 누군가 아버지 앞을 가로막으며 거칠게 끌어낸다고 했다. "난 한국으로 돌아가야 돼. 거기 내 가족이 있어. 제발, 보내줘. 일자리도, 이웃도, 내 청춘도 다 거기 두고 왔단 말이야. 제발……!" 잠꼬대 끝에 몸을 벌떡 일으키는 아버지는 매번 황급히 사방을 둘러본다. 그러고는 땀으로 흥건해진 속옷을 벗으며 어둠 속에서 긴 안도의 숨을 내쉰다.

그렇지만 나보다는 낫겠지. 난…… 태어난 곳은 있지만 고향이 없다. 한국에 네팔 대사관이 없어 아버지는 혼인신고를 못했다. 그래서 내겐 호적도 없고 국적도 없다. 학교에서조차 청강생일 뿐이다. 살아 있지만 태어난 적이 없다고 되어 있는 아이…….

깜빡 잠들었던 걸까. 눈을 뜨니 방 안이 어둑어둑하다. 눈을 비비고 밖으로 나간다. 오늘도 비재 아저씨는 감나무 밑에 앉아 먼 산을 바라보고 있다. 술이라면 한잔도 못 마시는 아저씨 얼굴이 이상스레 붉다. 마당 한

that I'd find the same happiness he does from the photos.

But in my eyes, the Himalayas in the afternoon sun looks like nothing more than a molar tooth capped with a gold crown. Or a creamy vanilla sundae about to melt on a hot day. The thick, black circle on the calendar is still caught in a whirlpool. Something isn't right with me these days. I can't seem to control my tongue. When I come home after a stressful day at school, everything frustrates me and I just get angry. Today, So-yeong's brother and his friends came down to my classroom at break time. I hid in the bathroom until class began. It's not him I was scared of. If he had come alone, I knew I could've taken him. But I definitely didn't want to be remembered as the kid who was ganged up on like a mouse. I don't think I could ever live with that.

The sunlight on the calendar has now shrunk to the size of a baby's palm. Any movement of the *pachhaura* startles the light and makes it quiver. A wave of drowsiness comes over me. How nice it would be to dream about going back home, like Father does each night. He says he dreams about returning to his village wearing an old *chumba*. Back

가운데 있는 수돗가는 사람들로 번잡하다. 쪼그리고 앉아 감자를 깎는 미얀마 아저씨 투라의 발등 위로 누군가 쌀뜨물을 하얗게 흘려보내고, 요란하게 뚝딱거리는 도마 위에선 양파와 피망과 호박이 다져진다. 꼬챙이에 꿰인 양고기가 팬 위에서 지지직 소리를 내며 노린내를 풍긴다. 발목에서 찰랑대던 어둠이 머리끝까지 차오르자, 감나무 가지에 걸린 백열등도 노랗게 빛을 발한다. 러시아 아가씨 마리나는 양동이에 덥힌 물을 세숫대야에 부어 금발의 긴 머리를 헹구고, 어린 토야는 저녁 짓는 엄마 등에 업혀 오랜만에 방긋방긋 웃는다. 온갖 나라 말과 온갖 음식 냄새가 뒤섞인 마당은 벌, 나비가 윙윙대는 야생화 꽃밭처럼 향기롭고 소란하다.

아버지는 보이지 않는다. 생일날까지도 야근을 하나 보다. 음식을 준비해야겠다. 고향을 느낄 만한 걸로. 그러면 아버지 맘도 누그러지겠지. 선반을 뒤져 양파와 감자, 저나콩 한 줌을 찾아낸다. 우선 저나콩을 물에 담가 불리고 감자와 양파 껍질을 벗겨 잘게 자른다. 네팔 버터 기우에 잘게 자른 재료를 넣고 살짝 볶은 다음 잠시 생각하다가 거럼메살라(여러 가지 양념을 말려 가루로 낸 것) 가루가 든 봉지를 꺼낸다. 봉지가 홀쭉하게 구겨

to the golden hills of slender tongue flowers and red rhododendron flowers from which the snow-covered mountains can be seen in the distance. Back to those familiar clay houses and friendly villagers. In the dreams, the golden, fiery flowers in front of his childhood home are in full bloom. When he steps into the yard, he is enveloped by family and friends. Together, they share a plentiful table of *dahl baht tarkari*, curried vegetables with rice and lentils, and grilled buffalo *choila* dressed in tomato and spices. When he tries to board the airplane the next day, he is blocked and dragged away. "I must return to Korea. My family needs me. Please, let me go. I left everything there—my job, my neighbors, my youth. Let me go!" This is when Father shoots up from bed. He checks his surroundings each time and realizes he had been sleep talking. He takes off his sweaty shirt and lets out a deep sigh into the darkness.

At least he *has* a place to call home. I have a birthplace but no homeland. My parents couldn't register their marriage here as there is no Nepal embassy in Korea. That's why I have no family register, not even a nationality. At school, I'm enrolled as an auditor. I'm a living child with no records of

져 있다. 거꾸로 들어 흔들어보니 바닥에만 남았던 가루가 조금 날린다. 지라와 랑, 쑥멜, 고추, 더니아 따위가 들어간 그 양념이 없으면 더르가리 맛을 제대로 낼 수 없다. 숟가락을 냄비에 푹 꽂고 가스불을 꺼버린다.

미래슈퍼에는 평소처럼 텔레비전이 크게 틀어져 있다. 며칠째 텔레비전 방송은 외국인 노동자에 관한 뉴스를 되풀이해 들려줬다. 내 고향 특산물 따위를 소개한 뒤 불법 체류 외국인을 강제 추방하겠다는 정부의 방침을 내보냈고, 시트콤을 통해 폭소를 퍼붓고 나서 방글라데시 출신 노동자가 열차에 몸을 던진 소식을 전했으며, 드라마와 토크쇼까지 끝난 자정 무렵에는 출국하는 외국인 노동자들로 붐비는 공항을 보여주었다. 너무 많이 듣다 보니 남의 일처럼 따분하게 느껴진다.

슈퍼마켓 한편에 놓인 간이탁자 주위에는 남자들이 둘러앉아 술을 마시고 있다. 바람이 이마를 건드리고 지나갈 때마다 소란스런 말소리가 들려온다. 한국어에다 러시아어와 영어, 네팔어까지 뒤섞인 그 기묘한 말은 내 고막을 건드리는 순간 한국어로 바뀌어 머릿속으로 미끄러져 들어온다. 그중에는 쿤도 앉아 있다. 쿤이

ever being born.

I guess I had fallen asleep. I wake up to a dark room. Rubbing my eyes, I step outside. Mr. Vijay is sitting under the persimmon tree again, gazing at the mountains. Though not one to drink alcohol, his face has a red glow to it. People are crowded around the communal sink area in the middle of the yard. Tura, the Burmese man, is peeling potatoes in a squatting position. Someone drains the milky water from the rice pot by Tura's feet. Onions, green peppers and squash are being chopped on the cutting board. The skewered lamb meat is sizzling in the pan and giving off a foul smell.

The darkness that had been lapping at our ankles has now crept up to the top of our heads, and the lightbulb hanging from the tree branch gives off a yellowish glow. Marina, the young girl from Russia, pours a bucket of water into a basin and proceeds to wash her long blonde hair. Baby Toya, wrapped around his mother's back while she prepares dinner, is all smiles for the first time in a long while. Languages and aromas from around the world mingle in the yard, like bumblebees and butterflies buzzing about a bed of wildflowers, busy and fragrant.

나를 알아보고 손짓한다. 가까이 다가가자 오징어 다리를 잘라 내 손에 쥐여 준다.

"러시안룰렛이야. 이번엔 팟의 손이, 다음엔 수언의 팔이 날아가는 거지." 몸집이 크고 얼굴이 시체처럼 하얀 우즈베키스탄 사람 세르게니는 손가락으로 권총 모양을 하고 맞은편에 앉은 이란 청년 샨에게 겨누면서 짓궂게 말한다. "맞아. 하지만 누구든 당일 점심까진 웃고 떠들지. 심지어 졸기까지 하고. 쿤 너도 일하다가 졸았지?" 윗 단추 두세 개를 풀어 가슴 털을 드러낸 샨은 소주를 입 속에 털어넣으며 맞장구친다. "나 졸지 않았어. 그냥 좀…… 딴생각은 했지만." 쿤은 눈을 크게 뜨고 고개를 흔든다. "마찬가지야. 기껏해야 마리나 생각이겠지. 아무튼 그러다 갑자기 자기 차례 맞는 거야. 덜컹." 세르게니는 손으로 권총 쏘는 시늉을 한다. 샨이 가슴을 감싸며 옆으로 푹 쓰러진다. 쿤은 남의 얘기 듣듯 낄낄거리며 웃는다. 그는 자기 앞에 놓인 소주병을 들어 필용이 아저씨 잔에 따른다. 머리카락이 빠져 정수리가 훤한 필용이 아저씨는 손사래 치며 취한 목소리로 말한다. "염병, 그만들 해라. 니들 쏠라대는 소리 땜에 내가 꼭 넘의 나라에 와 있는 거 같잖여. 니들, 이 나라

I don't see Father anywhere. He's probably working overtime—on his birthday no less. I guess I should start dinner—something that will remind him of home. That would be nice. I rummage the cupboards and find some onions, potatoes, and a handful of *chana* beans. While the beans soak in water, I peel the onions and potatoes and slice them. Then, I sauté them in *gheeu,* Nepalese butter. I stop to think what comes next and take out a bag of *garam masala,* various dried spices ground into a powder. The bag is heavily creased and looks empty. I turn it upside down and shake out what's left—only a puff of powder that had settled on the bottom. You can't make proper *tarkari* without *garam masala*, the cumin, cloves, cardamom, chilies, and coriander. I toss the spoon into the pot and turn off the stove.

As usual, the television is blaring at Mirae Supermarket. News stories about migrant workers have been making headlines for the past several days. The story starts by introducing some specialty Nepalese goods and then announces some new government plan to deport illegal residents. Then there's a story on the Bangladeshi migrant from the TV sitcom who threw himself in front of an on-

가 워떻게 오늘날 여기꺼정 왔는 줄 아냐? 옛날에 내가 공장에서 일할 땐 손가락은 유도 아녔어. 팔뚝이 날아가고 모가지가 뎅겅뎅겅 했으니까." 아저씨는 곧게 편 손을 목에 갖다 대고는 세게 내려치는 시늉을 한다. "첨엔 시골에서 올라온 촌뜨기들이라 멋모르고 일했지. 하긴, 먹고살기 힘들 때였으니까. 인제 한국 놈들은 이런 데서 일 안 혀. 막말로 씨발, 험한 일이니까 니들 시키지 존 일 시킬려고 데려왔간?" 옛날이 떠올라서인지 아니면 술기운이 돌아서인지 아저씨 얼굴이 벌겋게 달아올랐다. "아무리 그래도 안전장치는 해줘야죠." 세르게니가 오징어를 물어뜯으며 말한다. "늬들도 자르면 피 나오고 누르면 똥 나오는 사람이다, 이거냐? 웃기는 소리들 마. 한국 놈들한테도 안 해준 걸 늬들한테라고 해주겠냐? 아니꼬우면 돌아가. 젠장, 어차피 늬들도 고국으로 돌아가서 공장 차리고 사장되려고 여기 왔잖냐. 노동자들을 어떻게 다뤄야 되는지 눈 똑바로 뜨고 배워가. 다 산 교육이여." 비아냥대는 필용이 아저씨 말에 쿤이 시무룩한 표정을 짓자 이번에는 세르게니가 볼멘소리로 대꾸한다. "아무튼 돈도 좋지만 우린, 사람 대우, 그거 받고 싶어요. 돈 벌어 고향 간다고 해도 삼 년 겪은

coming train. Around midnight, when the TV dramas and talk shows are over, they air footage of the airport bustling with migrant workers. I've heard it all so many times that it no longer piques my interest.

A group of men are enjoying a few drinks around the folding table set up inside the mart. With every gust of wind that brushes past my forehead comes sounds of the men's raucous chatter. The instant the peculiar jumble of Korean, Russian, English and Nepalese hits my eardrums, it converts itself into Korean and enters my brain. Khun's there, too. He sees me and motions for me to come. He tears off a dried squid tentacle and hands it to me as I draw near.

"It's like Russian roulette. This time it's Paht's hand, next time it's gonna be Sayan's arm," says Sergeny, the heavy, pale-faced Uzbek. He makes a gun with his fingers and points it across the table at Sayan, the young Iranian whose top two buttons were undone, revealing his chest hair underneath.

"You're right," Sayan takes a shot of *soju* and chimes in. "But everything seems so fine and dandy in the morning. We even doze off sometimes. Khun, you fell asleep, didn't you?"

일 삼십 년 동안 악몽으로 남아 우릴 괴롭힐 거예요."

"맞아. 난 지금도 가끔 어릴 때 앞니 갈던 때 꿈을 꿔."

손가락으로 앞니를 가리키며 샨은 멋쩍게 웃는다.

오징어를 입에 물고 나는 유리창에 붙어 있는 글자들을 유심히 본다. Alladin 10달러. FirstClass 10달러. 그 옆에는 전화카드 사용 시간도 적혀 있다. 타일랜드 80, 스리랑카 47, 파키스탄 46, 사우디아라비아 50, 이란 70, 필리핀 80, 러시아 125. 물건을 고르는 것처럼 진열대를 죽 돌아본다. 온갖 종류의 과자와 빵, 강렬한 색채의 음료수가 눈 속으로 빨려 들어온다. 뱃속이 쓰리고 아프다.

"바윗고개 언덕을 홀로 너엄자니, 옛님이 그리워 눈물 납니다. 십여 년간 머슴살이 하도 서러워, 진달래꽃 안고서 눈물 납니다……" 필용이 아저씨가 무릎장단에 맞춰 노래 부른다. 고개를 숙이고 있던 쿤이 갑자기 입을 연다. "여기 올 때 진 빚도 다 못 갚았는데 이 꼴이 됐어. 고국에 돌아가봤자 손가락질밖에 기다리는 거 없으니……" 쿤의 눈길이 닿는 창밖으로 마을버스 한 대가 지나간다. 버스가 일으키는 바람에 전신주 옆에서 웃자란 고들빼기가 조용히 흔들린다. "마을을 빠져나오기 전에 만난 친척 아저씨 말이 생각나. 벼가 누렇게 익어

"I wasn't dozing off. I just had other things on my mind," Khun opens his eyes wide and shakes his head.

"Same difference. I bet you were thinking about Marina. Watch out. Before you know it, you'll be next. Bang!"

Sergeny pretends to fire the gun. Sayan clasps his chest and buckles over. Khun chuckles as if it was someone else's story. He picks up the bottle of *soju* in front of him and pours some into Mr. Piryong's cup.

Slightly drunk, the balding Mr. Piryong waves his hand back and forth and starts talking.

"Dammit, that's enough. Hearing you guys go off like that in your own languages makes *me* feel like I'm the foreigner here. Listen up, do you know how this nation got to where it is now? When I used to work in the factory, fingers were nothing. Whole forearms, chopped off. Necks dangling. Hanging by a thread." He pretends to chop his neck off with his hand.

"At first, we were all just a bunch of country bumpkins—we had no idea what we were in for. Times were tough back then, anyway. But today? Koreans would never work here. Fuck, they're giv-

가는 논길을 절름대며 걸어온 아저씨는 땀을 닦으며 말했지. 가지 마라. 내 절름대는 다리를 보고도 고향을 떠나겠다는 거야? 아녜요, 아저씨. 전 구르카 용병으로 전쟁터에 가는 게 아녜요. 전 한국으로 일하러 가요. 거긴 안전한 곳이냐? 아무렴요. 몇 년 일하고 돌아오면 시내에다 큰 가게 차릴 수 있어요. 그러고 나서 대나무다리를 건너 마을을 빠져나왔지. 가시나무 뜯는 산양 무리 옆을 지나, 마르샹디 강변을 따라 빠른 걸음으로 걸었어. 매 한 마리가 골짜기로부터 불어오는 바람을 타고 천천히 머리 위를 날더니 고향마을 쪽으로 날아가더군. 갑자기 다시 집으로 돌아갈까, 하는 생각이 들었지. 하지만 이미 돌이킬 수 없었어. 마침 내가 타야 할 타타버스가 먼지를 일으키며 달려오더군. 거역할 수 없는 운명, 카르마처럼……." 쿤의 물기 어린 눈을 보더니 샨도 덩달아 어린애처럼 울먹인다. "난 여기서 못된 짓을 너무 많이 했어. 그래서 집으로 못 돌아가. 나, 공장에서 주는 돼지고기 아주 많이 먹었어. 게다가 돼지 피로 만든 순대까지. 여기서는 문제없지만 고향에선 달라. 신 앞에 절을 하면서 죗값을 치러야 하는데…… 솔직히 무서워. 아무도 보지 않는 이곳에서라면 상관없지

ing you the hard jobs. You think they brought you over here to give you the good jobs?" His face is glowing—either because of the alcohol or because he was reminiscing.

"They should still make some kind of safety net," says Sergeny, biting off some squid.

"So you're saying you wanna be treated like people that bleed and shit just like the rest of us? Who are you kidding? You think they'd treat you any better than the Koreans who worked here? Otherwise, go back. Hell, y'all came here intending to go back and build your own factories, anyways. You better learn how to treat workers while you're at it. It's all living education."

At Mr. Piryong's cynical words, Khun glowers and Sergeny replies, "Money's important, but what we want is to be treated like people. True, we may go back after three years, but what we go through during that time will haunt us for the next thirty years."

"That's right. To this day I have dreams about grinding my front teeth as a child." Sayan points to his front teeth and lets out a nervous laugh.

I chew on the squid and look carefully at the letters on the window. Alladin $10. FirstClass $10. The

만……."

나는 칫솔, 치약, 고무줄, 면장갑 따위 잡화 진열대 앞을 지나 카운터 쪽으로 다가간다. 진열된 담배들 중에 하나 남은 네팔산 '수리예'를 면장갑 더미 뒤로 슬쩍 밀어넣는다. 그러고 나서 큰 소리로 묻는다.

"수리예는 없나요?"

언제나 뚱뚱한 배에 앞치마를 두르고 있는 주인아주머니가 쪽방에서 하품을 하며 나온다. 가짜 결혼을 해주고 외국인한테 매달 삼십만 원씩 받는 아주머니는 배가 전보다 더 나왔다.

"네팔 담배 말이냐?"

아주머니는 손등으로 입가를 닦으며 졸음기 섞인 목소리로 되묻는다. 나는 자신 있게 네, 라고 대답하고 나서 아주머니가 담배를 찾는 동안 거럼메살라 양념 봉지를 허리띠 안쪽에 쑤셔 넣는다. 그러고도 시간이 남아 쿠우 한 병을 잠바 안쪽 겨드랑이 사이에 끼운다. 숨이 멎는 것 같았지만 조금 지나니까 견딜 만하다.

"다른 담배는 안 돼?"

"요즘 아버지의 향수병이 심해서요. 꼭 네팔 담배를 피우고 싶대요. 그 냄새를 맡으면 고향의 가족들 곁에

phone card minutes are written on the side. Thailand 80, Sri Lanka 47, Pakistan 46, Saudi Arabia 50, Iran 70, Philippines 80, Russia 125. I survey the counter as if I'm trying to pick something out. Chips and crackers, bright-colored drinks get caught in my gaze. My stomach aches.

"Climbing this rocky hill alone," Mr. Piryong taps his knees and sings to the beat. "I cry for my long-lost love. Ten years of this farmhand life is sorrowful, indeed. Azaleas in my hand; tears down my face..."

Khun lifts his head and starts to speak. "I left my country with a load of debt. I'm no better off here than I was there. Even if I were to go back, the only thing waiting for me is pointed fingers..." A village bus drives by the window that Khun is gazing out of. A gust of wind from the bus's passing stirs up the overgrown greens by the utility pole.

"I still remember what the old villager said to me the day I left. He wiped his brow as he limped down the road lined with golden rice plants ready for harvesting. Don't leave, he said. You see me limping and you still want to go? No, sir, I'm not headed to the battlefields as a Gurkha soldier. I'm going to Korea to work. Is it safe there? Of course.

있는 것 같다면서."

　시키지도 않은 말을 늘어놓으며 거짓말을 보탠다. 그
때 마침 가게 문이 열리더니 진성 도장에 다니는 나딤
몰라가 안으로 들어온다. 키가 작고 눈썹 뼈가 심하게
튀어나온 그 인도 아저씨는 노랭이라고 불린다. 작년에
같은 공장에서 일하던 꾸빌이 심한 화상을 입고 죽었을
때 조의금은커녕 얼굴 한 번 내밀지 않았다고 해서 붙
여진 별명이다. 심지어 주변 사람들이 장례비를 모아
벽제 화장터로 간 일요일까지 그는 특근을 했다고 한
다. 그날, 아버지와 몇몇 주위 사람들은 뼛가루가 담긴
상자를 안고 어두워지는 공장 골목을 이리저리 걸어다
녔다. 고개를 숙이고 걷던 사람들은 사고가 난 공장 앞
에 멈춰 섰다. 입구를 막아놓았던 서너 개의 합판을 누
군가 발로 차 안쪽으로 넘어졌다. 갑자기 하늘에서 폭
우가 쏟아졌다. 사람들이 노래를 부르기 시작했다. 불분
명한 발음으로, 웅얼거리듯이, 그러다가 짐승들이 울부
짖듯이. 하지만 쏟아지는 비 때문에 노랫소리는 멀리 퍼
져나가지 못했고, 빗물처럼 시궁창으로 빨려 들어갔다.

　노랭이는 양손 가득 선물보따리를 들고 있다. 그는 내
일이면 고국으로 돌아간다며 입가에 흰 거품을 물고 신

Just a few years and I can come back and open a big store downtown. After I said goodbye, I crossed the bamboo bridge and left the village. I passed by the antelope herd nibbling at the thorn bushes and followed the Marshyangdi River, quickening my pace. Riding the valley wind, a falcon circled my head and flew toward my village, and I thought about going back right then. But there was no turning back. The TATA bus came racing in a cloud of dust. I guess you can't fight fate—it's like karma."

Seeing Khun's teary eyes, Sayan starts choking up, too, like a boy.

"I did too many bad things while I was here. That's why I can't go back. I ate a lot of pork at the factory. I even ate *soondae*, which has pig blood in it. There's nothing wrong with it here, but it's different at home. I'm going to have to pay for my sins when I face the gods... Honestly, I'm scared. I'm safe here where no one can see me..."

I walk past the shelves of toothbrushes, toothpaste, rubber bands, work gloves and other household goods and head towards the counter. I hide the one remaining pack of Surya, the Nepali cigarettes, behind the work gloves and call out in a

63

나게 떠들어댄다. 이 마을에 살면서 돈을 모아 귀국하는 사람을 보는 건 처음이다. 노랭이는 콜라 한 병과 소주 두 병을 들고 사람들이 둘러앉은 탁자로 다가가 선심 쓰듯 소리 나게 내려놓는다. "사람 안 같은 놈 꺼, 안 먹어." 누군가 소리치자 다들 자리에서 벌떡 일어나 밖으로 나가기 시작한다. 심지어 술이라면 환장하는 필용이 아저씨조차 휘청대며 뒤따라간다. 그들 뒤에 대고 노랭이가 소리친다. "사람 안 같은 건 니들이야, 새끼야. 언제까지고 돼지우리에서 살 거잖아. 난 고향 돌아가면 새 집 짓고 새 이불에서 잠잘 수 있어. 큰 가게도 차릴 거고. 알겠냐, 이 돼지새끼들아. 쿠달바차(개새끼)! 슈와레나차(돼지새끼)!"

세르게니가 몸을 획 돌리더니 주먹을 날린다. 노랭이는 탁자 위로 쓰러지고 병들이 바닥으로 내동댕이쳐진다. 깨진 병 조각과 술, 콜라 거품이 뒤섞여 가게 바닥이 어수선하다. 주인아주머니가 빗자루를 들고 나와 술꾼들 장딴지를 때리며 내쫓는다. "에구 지겨워. 이 노린내 나는 동네를 어서 떠야지." 아주머니는 바닥을 쓸면서 투덜거린다. 노랭이는 천천히 몸을 일으켜 입가의 피를 닦고 머리 모양을 매만진다. 그러고는 아무 일 없었다

loud voice.

"Are you all out of Surya?"

The storeowner, wearing an apron around her ever-bulging stomach, comes out yawning. After agreeing to marry a foreigner for 300,000 *won* a month, her stomach has grown even bigger.

"The Nepali cigarettes?"

She wipes her mouth with the back of her hand and asks in a half-sleepy voice. I respond with a confident yes and hide a bag of *garam masala* behind my belt as she looks for the cigarettes. I still have some time left, so I take one bottle of Qoo and stick it in my armpit under my jacket. I almost can't breathe for a few seconds, but I ease up soon after.

"Can't you buy another brand?" she asks.

"My father's very homesick these days, and he wants to smoke Nepali cigarettes. He says the smell makes it feel like he's with his family."

I add to the lie by telling her more than she asked for. The store door opens and Nadiim Mola from Jinseong Stamps walks in. Short with protruding brow bones, the Indian man is known as Weaselface around here. He earned that nickname last year, after Kubil's funeral. Kubil was a factory co-

는 듯이 가슴을 앞으로 내밀어 보이더니 쇼핑가방을 챙겨 쥔다. 가게를 나서려다 말고 그는 초콜릿을 집어 나에게 건넨다. 나는 고개를 젓는다. 그러자 내 턱 밑으로 가까이 들이밀며 한 번 더 권한다. 침이 꼴깍 넘어간다. 나는 입술을 꼭 다물고 더 세게 머리를 흔든다. 순간 노랭이 눈가가 붉어지더니 눈물이 맺힌다. 고름처럼 진한 눈물이다. 어쩔 수 없이 한쪽 손을 내미는 순간, 겨드랑이에 있던 쿠우 병이 바닥으로 떨어진다. 등짝이 서늘하고 식은땀이 난다. 재빨리 가게 밖으로 튀어나가 도망치는데 등 뒤에서 암고양이처럼 앙칼진 목소리가 쏟아진다. "야, 이 쥐새꺄, 어딜 도망가. 당장 네 애비를 이미그레이션에 고발할 테니 그런 줄 알아!"

진성 도장, 화진 스펀지, 원일 공업, 신광 유리, 동북 컨베이어 공업을 단숨에 지나친다. 가구단지 입구에서야 겨우 걸음을 멈춘다. 숨이 턱 밑까지 차올라 허리를 구부린 채 헉헉댄다. 목이 마르고 가슴이 활활 불타오른다. 흰 거품을 일으키며 쏟아지던 쿠우가 눈에 선하다. 핥아서라도 먹고 싶다.

공장 지붕 위로 뜬 희미한 달을 뒤로하고 나는 정처

worker who died of severe burns, and Nadiim didn't show up to the funeral or even offer a condolence gift. Even when Kubil's close friends visited the crematorium in Byeokjae with some money they collected to help with the funeral expenses, Nadiim worked overtime until Sunday. That day, Father and a few other friends held the box of ashes and walked up and down the factory alleys. Heads bent, the men stopped in front of the factory where the accident had taken place. Someone had kicked down the plywood boards blocking the entrance. An unexpected rain shower fell from the skies. The men started to sing. With indistinct accents, almost murmuring, then wailing like animals. But the pouring rain drowned out their voices. Their song fell into the sewers with the rainwater.

Weaselface is holding bags full of gifts in both hands. Spit froths at his lips as he excitedly shares that he is flying home tomorrow. He is the first person from this town who has earned enough to go back. He brings a bottle of Coke and two bottles of *soju* to the table where the men are sitting and sets them down as a showy gesture of his generosity.

"I don't take stuff from animals." With that, the

없이 걷는다. 가랑잎 하나가 사선을 그으며 팔랑팔랑 떨어져내린다. 날씨가 흐려지려나 보다. 아버지는 나한 테 나뭇잎 떨어지는 것을 보고 미리 날씨를 아는 법을 가르쳐주었다. 네팔에서 천문학을 공부하다 온 아버지 는 별이나 달을 보고 현재의 위치를 가늠할 줄 안다. 구름의 모양이나 색깔, 두께를 보고 날씨를 예측할 수도 있다. 그러나 아버지는 이곳에서 별을 연구하는 대신 전구를, 하루에 수백 개씩의 전구를 만들었다. 아침부 터 저녁까지 긴 대롱을 입에 대고 후, 후, 숨을 불어넣었 다. 매일매일 새로운 전구들이 세상의 어둠을 밝히기 위해 아버지 입술에서 태어났다. 그럴 때 아버지는 마 치 마술사처럼 보였다. 신기할 정도로 똑같은 크기, 찌 그러지지 않고 완전한 동그라미……. 그중에는 크리스 마스 나무를 장식하는 꼬마전구도, 간판 테두리에 촘촘 하게 박는 콩살구만 한 전구도 있었다. 지금보다 더 어 렸을 때 나는 아버지가 하는 일을 몹시 자랑스러워했 다. 어쩌다 동전이라도 손에 들어오면 풍선껌을 사서 아버지처럼 후후 방울을 불어댔다. 그러나 지금은 아니 다. 아버지의 폐에서 나와 입술 끝에서 내뱉는 바람으 로 만들어낸 전구들은 금세 아버지 곁을 떠나 휘황한

men get up and leave. Even Mr. Piryong, who would usually go crazy for alcohol, stumbles to follow the others out.

Weaselface yells at their backsides. "You're the ones living like animals. Are you going to stay in the pigsties forever? When I go back, I'm gonna build a new house and sleep with new blankets and open a big store, too. Did you hear that, you pigs? *Kkudal bajja! Syuwarenajja!*"

Sergeny turns around and punches Weaselface in the face. Weaselface falls onto the table and bottles drop all over the floor. The store floor is now in disarray with broken bottles, liquor, and foam. The storeowner appears with a broom and shoos the drunk men out.

"I'm sick and tired of this. I need to leave this putrid town." She grumbles as she sweeps up the mess.

Weaselface gets up slowly, wiping the blood from his mouth and fixing his hair. He puffs up his chest as if nothing had happened and grabs the shopping bags. He offers me some chocolate on his way out but I shake my head. He shoves the chocolate near my chin and insists. I gulp. I purse my lips and shake my head harder. Then, his eyes

백화점 건물에서, 거리의 간판에서, 혹은 야시장에서 환호성을 질러대듯 반짝였다. 그런 밤에도 아버지는 나달나달해진 폐를 쓰다듬으며 흐린 형광등 아래로 기어들어왔다. 아버지한테서는 짐승 냄새가 났다. 땀과 화학약품과 욕설에 전, 종일 쉬지 않고 일한 몸뚱이가 풍기는 고약한 단내.

어머니는 언제나 한국말로 아버지에게 따졌다. 마치 송곳에라도 찔린 사람처럼 가늘고 날이 선 목소리로, 아버지는 가슴을 움켜쥐었다. 아버지는 말을 더듬거렸고 숨이 차 헐떡였다. 그러면 다시 어머니가 가래가 튀어나올 정도로 목청을 높였다. 어머니는 돈도 제대로 못 버는 아버지와 의료보험조차 없는 처지를 견디기 힘들어했다. 언제나 한국 남자와 혼인해서 잘살고 있다는 친구 얘기를 끄집어내면서 신세 한탄을 했다. 내가 감기에라도 걸리면 어머니는 내 등짝을 후려쳤다. "그러니까 밤에 잘 때 이불을 걷어차지 말랬잖아. 병원 한 번 갔다 오려면 몇 만 원이 깨진다구. 벌써 석 달째 월급이 밀렸어. 이젠 정말 지긋지긋해!" 하면서 차가운 물수건을 내 이마에 철퍼덕 얹었다. 그런 어머니가 십 년 전엔 열이 펄펄 나는 아버지 이마를 부드러운 손길로 짚어줬

redden and fill with tears. Fat, pus-like tears. Feeling bad, I reach out my hand to accept his gift, at which time the bottle of Qoo that I'd been hiding in my armpit falls to the floor. Chills run down my spine and I break out into a cold sweat. I bolt out of the store and run away but cat-like shrieks fly after me. "You lil' rat! How dare you run away? I'm gonna report your dad to immigration this instant, you hear?"

I run past Jinseong Stamps, Hwajin Sponge, Wonil Industrial, Shingwang Glass, and Dongbuk Conveyor Industrial in what seems like one breath. I finally stop at the entrance of the furniture complex. My heart is pounding and I bend over panting. My throat is parched and my chest is burning. I visualize the spilled bottle of Qoo, white fizz and all. I'd lick it up if I could.

I turn my back to the hazy moon above the factory rooftops and walk. A leaf flutters to the ground at a diagonal. Perhaps the clouds are coming. Father taught me how to predict the weather by noting how the leaves fall. Having studied astronomy in Nepal, he can use the moon and the stars to position himself. He can even read the shape, color

다니. 한때 연보랏빛 말링고꽃처럼 예뻤었다니. 아버지 말이 도저히 믿어지지 않는다.

기침이 멈추지 않아 아버지는 할 수 없이 직장을 옮겼다. 아버지의 새 직장은 상자를 만드는 곳이다. 아버지는 아침부터 저녁까지 무거운 종이를 어깨에 지고 나른다. 기계에서 칼선대로 찍혀 나온 종이는 컨베이어 벨트 위에서 주스 상자가 되고 종합선물세트 상자가 되고 고급 와이셔츠 상자가 되었다. 그것들을 백화점에 보내면 속에 내용물이 담겨 진열된다고 한다. 나는 한 번도 백화점에 가보지 못했다. 작년 겨울에 아버지와 어머니 생일 전날 백화점에 찾아간 적이 있는데 입구에 서 있는 양복쟁이 아저씨가 앞을 가로막았다. 아버지는 지갑에서 돈을 꺼내 보여주며 나 돈 있어요, 여기 봐요, 나도 물건 살 거예요, 라고 말했지만 양복쟁이는 막무가내였다. 그날 우리는 결국 어머니가 바라던 고급 블라우스를 사지 못했다. 어머니가 기어코 아버지 곁을 떠난 건 그 때문일까.

긴 생머리를 고무줄로 대충 묶은 채 옆방 토야 엄마랑 종일 나사를 끼우던 어머니는 그즈음부터 원당 시내에 있는 식당으로 일하러 나갔다. 얼마쯤 지나자 어머

and thickness of clouds to predict the weather, too.

But, here, instead of studying the stars, Father made hundreds of light bulbs a day. He would blow into a long tube day and night. New bulbs were born out of his mouth to bring light to darkness. He looked like a magician when he did that. It was amazing how they came out the same size, in perfect circles, without a single dent... He made mini bulbs for Christmas tree lights and green apricot-sized bulbs to frame billboards, too. When I was a lot younger than I am now, I used to be really proud of what he did. Whenever I got my hands on some change, I'd buy bubblegum and blow bubbles to imitate him.

Not anymore though. The light bulbs that got filled with the air from Father's lungs exiting his lips ended up in resplendent department store buildings, street signs, and night markets, dazzling in the darkness. Meanwhile, Father would come home clenching his chest where his worn-out lungs were, and crawl under the fluorescent light. He smelled like an animal. It was the rancid smell of sweat and chemicals and swear words after a long day of work with no breaks.

니는 구슬 박힌 핀이며 실크 스카프 따위가 담긴 예쁜 상자를 집으로 가져왔다. 손가락을 세워 입술에 갖다 대며 어머니는 내게 눈을 찡긋, 했다. 누구한테서든 그런 선물을 받을 수 있다면, 그래서 어머니가 더 행복해진다면 좋겠거니 생각한 나는 그 일을 아버지한테 말하지 않았다. 하지만 선물상자가 쌓일수록 어머니는 점점 더 신경질을 부려댔고 분첩으로 사정없이 얼굴을 두드려댔다.

집을 나가던 날 아침에 어머니는 모시조개를 넣은 미역국을 끓였다. 국 한 그릇을 다 비우고 좀 더 달라고 하자 어머니는 저녁에 실컷 먹으라며 어서 학교에 가라고 등을 떠밀었다. "오늘 어디 가?" 왜 그렇게 물었는지 모르겠다. 그냥 그런 생각이 들었다. 오후에 집에 와보니 어머니가 없었다. 대신 미역국이 한 솥 끓여져 있었다. 나는 일찌감치 저녁을 먹고 잠자리에 들었다. 어머니를 기다리지 않았는데, 왜 그랬는지 모르겠다. 그냥…… 기다려도 소용없을 것 같았다. 그렇지만 깊이 잠들지는 못했다. 야근하는 아버지 공장에서 나오는 덜컥대는 기계 소리가 바람벽을 뚫고 밤새 들려와 내내 벼랑에서 떨어지는 꿈을 꾸어야 했다.

Mother constantly nagged at him in Korean. She behaved as though she had been stabbed by an awl—her shrill and piercing words twisted his heart. Father stammered when he replied, sounding out of breath. This made her raise her voice so high that the phlegm almost came flying out of her throat. Mother found it hard to be happy with her circumstances. Her husband didn't make enough money and she didn't even have health insurance. She lamented her fate as she frequently talked about friends who married Korean men and were doing well.

Once, when I came down with a cold, she gave me a good smack on my back. "Didn't I tell you not to throw off the blanket at night? One trip to the doctor is more than ten thousand *won* down the drain. It's been three months since your father has been paid. I can't stand this anymore!" She dropped a cold, wet hand towel on my forehead. It's hard to believe she was the same woman who sweetly tended to her fever-ridden husband ten years ago. That she was as beautiful as a lilac-colored *malingo* flower. Very hard, indeed.

Father's cough wouldn't go away so he had to switch jobs. His new job was making cardboard

가구단지로 접어드니 사방이 휘황하다. 온갖 종류의 전구와 네온사인이 켜져 있다. 보루네오, 리바트, 대진 침대, 이태리가구 앞을 지난다. 전시장마다 내걸린, '수입 명품 특별전' '고급 엔틱 가구 할인'이라고 쓰인 플래카드가 습기 품은 바람에 들썩댄다. 통유리 안쪽에는 크고 화려한 침대며, 콘솔, 소파 따위가 멋지게 진열되어 있다. 고급스런 옷을 입은 아주머니들이 그 사이로 걸어다니고, 양복 차림의 젊은 남자들은 가구를 보여주거나 종이에 뭔가 쓴다. 문득 가구공장에서 일하는 비재 아저씨와 3호실의 낡아빠진 캐비닛, 총탄에 맞은 것처럼 구멍 뚫린 벽, 그리고 땅에 매여 우주를 떠받치고 있는 코끼리의 짓눌린 등이 떠오른다. 가당치도 않다. 저 사람들하고 신세를 비교하다니. 나는 고개를 설레설레 흔들면서 유리문 안쪽 세계에서 눈을 돌린다. 허리춤에 손을 대보니 거럼메살라 봉지가 만져진다. 마음이 뿌듯하다. 양말이라도 하나 예쁘게 포장해 아버지께 드린다면 더 좋겠지만 그러려면 문방구에 들어가 또 훔쳐야 한다. 그렇게까지 하고 싶지는 않다.

큰길에서 벗어나 골목으로 들어선다. 미래슈퍼 앞을

boxes. From morning to evening, he hauled heavy cardboard on his shoulders. After a machine cuts the cardboard along the marked lines, it is moved to a conveyor belt where it becomes juice boxes, gift boxes, and high-end dress shirt boxes. They then get sent to department stores where they are filled and put on display. I've never been inside a department store before. On the day before Mother's birthday last winter, Father and I were stopped by a suited man at the entrance. Father took out his wallet and tried to convince the man, "See? I have the money. I can pay!" It was to no avail. In the end, we couldn't buy the high-end blouse that Mother wanted. I wonder if that's why she ended up leaving him.

It was around then that Mother started working at a restaurant in downtown Wondang. Until then, she had spent her days with her long black hair sloppily tied, working with Toya's mom next door attaching screws. Not long after her new job, she came home with a pretty box containing a beaded hair pin and a silk scarf. Sensing my curiosity, she winked at me. I decided not to tell Father, thinking that as long as she kept receiving these gifts, she'd be happier. As the gift boxes started piling up,

지나지 않고도 집으로 돌아갈 수 있는 이 길은 전에 친구와 와본 적이 있어 낯익다. 어둠이 짙다. 더듬듯이 한발 한발 내딛는데도 웅덩이에 발이 빠져 넘어질 뻔했다. 그래도 어지러운 네온 불빛보다는 고른 어둠이 낫다. 가망 없는 인정을 기대하는 것보다 도둑질을 할 수 있는 강한 심장을 갖는 게 더 나은 것처럼. 아버지는 미친 듯이 빛을 뿜는 네온사인은 단 하나의 그림자도 만들지 못한다고 늘 못마땅해했다. 아버지는 언제나 푸른 달빛을 그리워했다. 밤이면 만병초 그림자를 땅 위에 가지런히 뉘어놓고 세상을 휴식하게 한다는 히말라야의 달빛……. 오늘 밤엔 왠지 나도 그런 달빛이 보고 싶다.

골목 모퉁이 은밀한 곳에 다다르자 빅토리아 관광나이트클럽 포스터가 붙어 있다. 어슴푸레한 가로등 불빛 아래 벗은 마리나 모습이 도드라진다. 젖가슴을 반 이상 드러낸 까만 브래지어와 반짝이 팬티를 입은 마리나는 엉덩이 뒤쪽으로 공작꼬리처럼 생긴 화려한 인조 깃털을 매달고 있다. 대리석처럼 하얗고 긴 팔다리는 압사라 춤을 추듯 기묘하게 꼬여 있다. 금발 머리를 틀어 올리고 입술을 빨갛게 칠해 쉽게 알아볼 수 없게 분장

however, she became crabbier and powdered her face like it was her job.

On the morning she left for good, Mother cooked a pot of *miyeokguk* with short-necked clams. I emptied my bowl of the seaweed soup and asked for more, but she said I could have as much as I want at dinner and hurried me off to school. "Are you going somewhere today?" I don't know what prompted me to ask. I just had a feeling. When I came home later that afternoon, she wasn't there. Instead, there was a pot of new *miyeokguk* on the stove. I ate dinner early that day and went to bed. I didn't wait for her—I don't know why. I just... I didn't think waiting would change anything. Still, I couldn't fall into a deep sleep. The rattling of the machines from the factory where Father was working late penetrated the wall into my ears all night long and I dreamt I was falling off a cliff.

I turn into the furniture complex and there are dazzling lights everywhere. All sorts of light bulbs and neon signs flash their lights. I walk past Borneo, Livart, Daejin Bed, and Italian Furnishings. The nylon placards plastered with "Special Sale on Luxury Imports," "Discounted Luxury Antiques" strung in front of the exhibitions flap in the humid wind.

했지만 그녀의 보랏빛 눈동자만은 숨길 수가 없다. "꼬마야, 이름이 뭐니?" 그녀는 축사 건물로 이사 온 며칠 뒤에 수돗가에서 내게 말을 걸어왔다. "아카스예요. 네팔 말로 하늘이란 뜻이래요." "그래? 내 이름은 마리나. 러시아어로 바다란 뜻이야. 파란 하늘, 파란 바다……." 입술을 달싹이며 그 말을 되풀이하던 마리나는 하바로프스크에 살고 있는 어머니와 여동생 카타리나, 그리고 죽은 아버지 이야기를 들려줬다. 어릴 적에 온 가족이 집 둘레에 사과나무와 체리나무, 슬리바나무를 심던 이야기, 주말이면 근교까지 자전거를 타고 가 숲에서 송이버섯을 따던 이야기, 유치원에서 아이들에게 춤과 노래를 가르치던 때 이야기도 들려주었다. 꿈꾸듯 빛나던 그녀의 보랏빛 눈동자는 그러나 아버지가 체첸 전쟁에서 죽고 혼자 생계를 책임지던 어머니마저 병들어 한국행 배를 탔다는 말을 하면서부터 깊은 바닷물처럼 일렁였다.

나는 마리나 배꼽 주변에 누군가 묻혀놓은 검은 얼룩을 손으로 닦아준다. 얼룩은 잘 지워지지 않고 대신 종이가 찢어진다. 마리나는 상처가 난 채 억지로 웃는 것 같은 이상한 모습이 되어버렸다. 갑자기 바람이 거세게

Giant, fancy beds, console tables, and sofas are lavishly arranged behind the thick, glass windows. Well-dressed women meander their way around them while suited young men show off the furniture or jot things down on paper.

Images suddenly flash across my mind: Mr. Vijay, who works at a furniture factory; Room 3 with the worn cabinets and what looks like bullet-ridden walls; the elephant tied to the ground with the weight of the universe on his back. It is so unfair. How could I compare my lot with the people in the store? Shaking my head, I turn my gaze away from the world behind those glass doors. I remember the bag of *garam masala* against my waist and feel proud of myself. It would've been nice to give Father a nicely wrapped pair of socks, too, but then I'd have to go to the stationary shop and steal again. I don't want to do that.

I turn into an alley off the main road. This route ensures that I don't have to pass Mirae Supermarket to go home. I had taken this shortcut once with a friend so it looks familiar. The darkness is heavy. I take care with each step but I trip over a pothole and almost lose my balance. Still, I'd take the im-

분다. 담장을 넘은 정원수들이 딸꾹질을 하며 나뭇잎을 떨어뜨린다.

조금 더 걸어가니 빨간 벽돌로 지은 이층집이 보인다. 치아처럼 부드러운 빛이 커튼을 뚫고 흘러나온다. 난생처음 반 친구한테 초대받아 갔던 바로 그 집이다. 어느 날 그 애는 자기 집에 같이 가겠느냐는 뜻밖의 말을 했다. 그 말을 하고 나서 그 애는 누가 볼까 봐 겁내는 듯한 표정으로 사방을 둘러보았다. 그러고는 못 알아들은 것 같은 멍한 얼굴을 하고 있는 내게 바짝 다가와 귀에 대고 낮게 속삭였다. 아니, 작지만 몹시 퉁명스런 말을 내동댕이쳤다. 우리 엄마가 너더러 한번 들르래. 그 애는 열 발자국쯤 앞서서 걸으며 가끔 내가 잘 따라오고 있는지 확인했다. "헬로, 나이스 투 미튜." 친구 어머니는 빨갛게 칠해진 얇은 입술을 실지렁이처럼 꿈틀댔다. 잇몸을 드러내며 크게 웃는 입과 차고 날카로운 눈이 묘하게 합해진 얼굴이었다. 우물쭈물하다가 안녕하세요, 라고 인사를 했다. 그러자 아줌마 표정이 일그러졌다. "너 영어를 잘 못하니? 외국 애라고 해서 영어를 잘하는 줄 알았는데." 아주머니는 이제부터 영어로만 말하라고 했다. 그러지 않으면 떡볶이와 스파게티를 주지

partial darkness over the dizzy neon lights any day. It's like how being brave enough to steal is better than hoping for acceptance I'll never get. Father always looked disapprovingly at those crazy flashing neon lights, saying that they were incapable of casting any shadows. Father longed for the blue moonlight—the Himalayan moonlight that laid the rhododendron shadows to bed and gave the world rest. Oddly tonight, I want to see that moonlight, too.

I come to a covert bend and see a poster for Victoria Nightclub on the lamppost. Marina's bare figure stands out under the dim light. Dressed in glittering panties and a dark brassiere exposing half of her breasts, she is also wearing a waist-piece of large, showy artificial feathers resembling a peacock's tail. Her long, marble-white arms and legs are peculiarly crossed, like she's doing the Apsara dance. With her blonde hair in a bun and lips stained bright red, her makeup made it hard to tell who she was, but her amethyst-colored eyes gave her away.

"What's your name, little one?" A few days after she moved in to the livestock building, she saw me by the communal sinks and started a conversation.

않겠다면서. 떡볶이와 스파게티……. 고통스러울 정도로 속이 쓰리고 아프다. 그 애나 아줌마나 다 맘에 들진 않지만, 그래도 초인종을 누르고 싶다. 지난번처럼 영어 몇 마디를 가르쳐주면 뭐든 얻어먹을 수 있지 않을까.

키 큰 풀들이 흔들리고 있는 공터를 지난다. 말라가는 풀 냄새와 분뇨 냄새가 풍겨온다. 공터 여기저기에 함부로 버려져 있는 냉장고와 부서진 의자, 자질구레한 플라스틱 잡동사니들 위로 호박덩굴이 무성하다. 허름한 집 몇 채가 늘어선 골목을 지나니 누군가 노래를 부르며 걸어오는 게 보인다. 어두워서 잘 보이지는 않지만 작은 키에다 양손에 쇼핑백을 든 걸 보니 노랭이가 분명하다. 갑자기 가슴이 뛰기 시작한다. 공터 옆으로 난 산길로 더 많이 돌아서 가야겠다. 산길로 접어드는데 발밑에 뭔가 걸린다. 무성하게 자란 호박덩굴이다. 늦가을까지 남아 노끈처럼 질겨진 덩굴은 내 발목을 휘감고는 놓아주지 않는다. 엉덩이를 바닥에 대고 주저앉아 덩굴을 푼다. 노랫소리는 점차 가까이 다가오더니 공터 쪽으로 다시 멀어진다. 그때, 버려진 냉장고 뒤에서 검은 물체가 솟아오른다. 검은 물체는 빵처럼 점점

"Akash. It means 'sky' in Nepali."

"Is that right? Mine's Marina. It means 'from the sea' in Russian. The blue sky, the blue sea..."

After mouthing our names again, she told me about her mother in Havarovsk, her younger sister Katarina, and her deceased father. She told me how the whole family planted apple trees and cherry trees around their house when she was young, and how she would bike to the outskirts of town and pick mushrooms in the woods. How she taught children songs and dances at the kindergarten. Her lavender eyes danced as she recounted her younger days. But when she started talking about the Chechen War, her eyes tossed like the waves. Her father had died in the war, leaving her mother to feed the family alone. And when her mother fell ill, Marina boarded a boat for Korea.

Somebody had smeared something black on the poster near Marina's belly button. It is hard to wipe off and the paper tears. Marina now looks like she is forcing a smile despite being wounded. A sudden gust of wind blows. The trees in the garden over the wall hiccup and let go of some of their leaves.

I walk a little further and see the two-story brick

부풀어오른다. 노랭이는 더 빠른 박자로 노래한다. 검은 물체가 소리 없이 노랭이 뒤를 따른다. 픽 소리와 함께 노랫소리가 뚝 끊긴다. 검은 물체는 쓰러진 노랭이 앞가슴에서 심장을 뜯어내듯 지갑을 뺏는다. 희미한 달빛 아래 입을 벌리고 웃는 얼굴이 얼핏 보인다. 비재 아저씨다. 나는 눈을 질끈 감는다. 눈꺼풀 안쪽으로 은색 코끼리 한 마리가 나타난다. 구덩이에 발이 빠진 코끼리는 큰 귀를 펄럭이며 빠져나오려고 안간힘을 쓰고 있다. 하지만 발버둥 칠수록 뒷다리는 점점 더 깊이 빨려들어간다. 구덩이는 삽시간에 시커먼 늪으로 변하더니 뭐든 집어삼킬 태세로 거세게 휘돌아간다. 아, '외'다. 현기증이 일도록 빠르게 소용돌이치는 '외…….' 코끼리는 맥없이 빨려 들어간다. 미처 비명을 지르지 못하고 눈을 부릅뜬 채. 눈앞이 온통 까맣다.

「코끼리」, 실천문학사, 2005

house. A light, warm like *chiya* tea, seeps through the curtains and streams out. My classmate lives there—nobody had ever invited me over but him. One day, out of the blue, he asked if I wanted to come over. He looked around, worried, it seemed, that someone else might've heard. Seeing my blank stare, he whispered into my ear. Quietly but bluntly, he said, "My mom wants you to come." He walked about ten paces ahead of me and looked over his shoulder from time to time to make sure I was following along.

"Hello, nice to meet you." His mom's bright red lips wriggled like worms. Her big smile exposed her gums and her cold, sharp eyes made for a peculiar face. Not knowing how to respond, I said, "*Annyeonghaseyo.*"

She made a face at me, saying, "You don't speak English? I thought all foreigners were good at English." She instructed us to only speak in English from that point forward. Otherwise, we wouldn't be allowed to eat the *tteokbokki* and spaghetti she had prepared. *tteokbokki* and spaghetti... My stomach now reels in hunger. I don't like the kid or his mom, but I'm still tempted to ring the doorbell. I figure, if I teach him a few things in English, I could eat whatever I ask for.

I walk past the vacant lot where the overgrown grasses sway in the wind. I can smell the drying grass and manure. Strewn about the lot are an old refrigerator, a broken chair, and a bunch of plastic odds and ends, on top of which lie thick pumpkin vines tangled about. As I pass a street of shabby houses, I hear someone singing.

It's getting louder. I make out a short man carrying shopping bags in both hands and I'm sure it's Weaselface. My heart starts pounding. I decide to take a detour through the mountain trail. As I turn into the trail, my foot gets caught on something. It's an overgrown pumpkin vine. The rope vine, having lasted until late autumn, has grown leathery and wraps itself around my ankle, refusing to let go. I park my rear on the ground and try to free my foot.

The singing gradually draws nearer and then heads farther towards the lot. Then, a black figure emerges from behind the refrigerator, rising like bread in the oven. Weaselface's song speeds up. The black figure follows Weaselface without a sound. There is a wham! and the singing stops. The black figure rips the wallet from Weaselface's chest pocket. It's as if his heart was being torn out. I catch a glimpse of the figure's mouth wide open, laughing under the hazy moonlight. It's Mr. Vijay. I shut my eyes tight.

A silver elephant appears on my inner eyelids. The elephant's foot is stuck in a pothole and his big ears flap as he tries to free himself. But the harder he tries, the deeper his back leg sinks. The pothole turns into a blackish swamp that starts to whirl violently, swallowing everything around it. Ah, it's *oue*. Spinning 'round and 'round. It's dizzying. Helpless, the elephant is sucked in. Not one sound comes out of him; his eyes remained wide open. My own world turns black.

Translated by Michelle Jooeun Kim

해설

Afterword

신자유주의와 디아스포라의 삶

고봉준 (문학평론가)

　　산업자본주의 시기에 한국은 세계 전역으로 노동력
을 수출하는 신흥 개발국의 하나였으나, 신자유주의가
지구 전체를 장악한 현재 한국은 세계적인 노동력 수입
국의 일원이 되었다. 신자유주의의 도래는 자본의 전
(全)지구적 이동과, 자본의 흐름을 따라 움직이는 노동
력의 대량 이주라는 현상을 낳았고, 이는 과거 식민주
의 시기와는 다른 의미에서 광범위한 노동의 디아스포
라 현상을 촉진하고 있다. 이러한 변화는 국내 노동시
장의 성격에 커다란 변화를 가져왔다. '노동'과 '자본'의
선명한 갈등과 대립이 희미해지는 대신 정규직과 비정
규직, 내국인 노동자와 외국인 노동자 간의 갈등과 문

Neoliberalism and Life in Diaspora

Ko Bong-jun (literary critic)

During its period of industrial capitalism, Korea was just one of many newly developing countries exporting labor across the world. The Korea of today, however, has become a major power in the neoliberal world and has become an importer of global labor forces. The advent of neoliberalism gave birth to the labor migration phenomenon, a trend in which capital moves across the planet and the labor force moves with it. This has spurred a widespread labor diaspora phenomenon, different from the old colonial era, changing the domestic labor market greatly. While the lines between "labor" and "capital" have become blurred, new con-

화의 충돌이라는 새로운 현상이 생긴 것이다. 김재영의 『코끼리』는 한국의 중소업체에서 열악한 노동환경에 신음하는 이주노동자들의 비참한 삶을 그린 상징적인 작품 가운데 하나로 노동력의 디아스포라가 산출하는 참상과 다문화주의 이데올로기로는 설명될 수 없는 노동에 대한 자본의 착취 문제를 정면으로 고발하고 있다.

이 소설의 공간적 배경인 '식사동 가구공단'은 신자유주의 시대를 살아가는 지구의 축소판이다. 네팔, 중국, 파키스탄, 방글라데시, 미얀마, 러시아, 베트남, 이란, 스리랑카, 우즈베키스탄, 인도 등 신자유주의 체제의 주변 국가에서 온 이방인들이 이 위성도시의 을씨년스러운 가구 공간에서 함께 살아간다. 심지어 주인공 '나'가 살고 있는 "십여 년 전까지 돼지축사로 쓰였다는, 낡은 베니어판 문 다섯 개가 나란히 붙어 있는 건물"마저도 다국적 전시장을 연상시킨다. 1호실의 미얀마 아저씨들, 2호실의 방글라데시 아주머니, 3호실의 비재 아저씨, 4호실의 '나'와 아빠, 5호실의 러시아 아가씨는 모두 국적이 다르다. 그럼에도 불구하고 이들 사이에는 분명한 공통점이 한 가지 있는데, 그것은 이들 모두가 거대한 '외', 즉 '소용돌이'에 빠졌다는 것이다. "1호실 미얀마

flicts now face both full-time and part-time, Korean and non-Korean working people in the form of culture clashes. "The Elephant," by Kim Jae-young is a symbolic piece about the harsh life of migrant workers working under dangerous and unsanitary working conditions of small and medium-sized enterprises in Korea. It raises charges against the labor exploitation, an issue that cannot be fully explained by the horrors of labor diaspora and the ideology of multiculturalism.

The physical setting of this story, the furniture complex in Siksa-dong, is a small-scale planet during the neoliberal era. Migrants from Nepal, China, Pakistan, Bangladesh, Myanmar, Russia, Vietnam, Iran, Sri Lanka, Uzbekistan, and India all live in the dreary industrial complex located in this satellite city. Even the building lined by "the five worn veneer doors" that "used to be a pig shed up until about ten years ago" and houses the main character Akash is a multinational exhibit. The occupants are diverse—the Myanmar men in Room 1, the Bangladeshi woman in Room 2, Mr. Vijay in Room 3, Akash and his father in Room 4, and the young Russian lady in Room 5. However, what they all share in common is that they are caught in a

아저씨들은, 한국에 온 외국인 노동자들은 모두 '외'에 빠진 거라고 말한다." '외'란 무엇일까? '악마의 맷돌'이 다. 그것은 개인의 의지와 노력으로는 도저히 벗어날 수 없는 불가항력의 힘, 구체적으로는 자본주의적 현실 과 신체 절단, "시퍼런 멍과 상처"와 분리할 수 없는 비 참한 노동 현실, 그러니까 바닥을 알 수 없는 삶의 추락 을 의미한다. 주인공 '나'는 "구름보다 높은 히말라야에 서 태어나 이곳, 후미진 공장지대에서 살아가고" 있는 아버지를 신화 속의 '코끼리'와 동일시하지만, "히말라 야 달력 사진"은 심리적인 위안은 될지언정 현실적인 구원은 되지 못한다. 이들의 삶이 소용돌이를 벗어날 수 없는 또 하나의 이유는 '식사동 가구공단'이 표면적 인 유대의 저변에 철저한 자본주의적 삶의 태도를 숨기 고 있기 때문이다. 그것은 한 마디로 생존을 위해서라 면 타인의 상처와 희생 따위는 생각하지 않는 비정한 정글의 법칙이다. 작품의 초반부에서 3호실의 비재 아 저씨는 파키스탄 청년 알리에게 전 재산을 도둑맞지만, 결말부에서 그 또한 강도로 돌변하여 귀국을 앞둔 노랭 이를 공격한다. 뿐만 아니라 13살의 '나'는 아버지의 생 일선물을 마련한다는 명목으로 아무런 가책 없이 가게

"whirlpool," the devil's millstone. This refers to an unassailable power that cannot be overcome by individual will or strength, the capitalist and labor-related realities leading to accidental amputations, blackened eyes, bruises and scars. Falling into despair. Akash compares his father—who was born above the clouds in the Himalayas, but now only works in a remote factory district—to the elephant in Hindu mythology. The Himalaya picture calendar may provide some psychological solace to the homesick migrants but it cannot save them from reality.

Hidden under the surface-level bonds at Siksa-dong are the irrefutable facts of capitalist life, a life that operates according to the cold-hearted law of the jungle, eat or be eaten. In the beginning of the story, Mr. Vijay from Room 3 is robbed of his entire savings by Ali, a Pakistani teenager. By the end of the story, however, Mr. Vijay turns into a thief himself, attacking the homebound Weaselface. Not only that, Akash brazenly shoplifts for his father's birthday dinner, justifying it as a good deed for his father. The migrants in Siksa-dong are entrapped in this ruthless whirlpool in part because they accept capitalistic laws of survival. This is perfectly in

에서 물건을 훔치며, 심지어 도둑질을 위해서 아버지에 대한 자식의 호의를 팔기도 한다. 그러므로 '식사동 가구공단'에서 일하는 외국인 노동자들이 헤어날 수 없는 소용돌이에 빠지는 데는 자본주의적 생존법칙을 받아들인 그들의 몫도 존재하는 바, 그것은 "가망 없는 인정을 기대하는 것보다 도둑질을 할 수 있는 강한 심장을 갖는 게" 더 낫다는 '나'의 생존본능과 한 치도 어긋나지 않는다. 김재영의 소설이 상대적으로 아시아 국가를 순수하고 신비로운 곳으로 표상함으로써 아시아와 한국을 '선'과 '악'의 대립으로 인식한다는 지적도 없지 않다. 하지만 그의 소설은 "살아 있지만 태어난 적이 없다고 되어 있는 아이"인 '나'의 존재를 통해 살아 있는 주검의 상태를 벗어나기 어려운 이주노동자의 존재론적 위치를 적확하게 포착하고 있으며, 신자유주의하에서 사회의 극단적인 주변으로 내몰리는 노동자—디아스포라의 불행한 삶, 그리고 한 사회의 가장자리에서 살아가는 사람들에게 행해지는 극단의 폭력적 현실에 주목한다는 점에서 지구화 시대에 대한 문학적 대응으로 평가할 가치가 있다.

line with Akash's survival instinct: "being brave enough to steal is better than hoping for acceptance I'll never get."

There are some that critique Kim Jae-young's depictions of Asian countries except for Korea as being too pure and mysterious, portraying Korea and the rest of Asia as caught in a sort of conflict between good and evil. However, by focusing on Akash's existence, "a living child who has no records of ever being born," the novel accurately captures the existential position of migrant workers who are sometimes nothing more than living corpses.

"The Elephant" is also worth evaluating as a literary response to globalization. It focuses on the unfortunate lives of the laborer-diaspora pushed to the fringes of society under neoliberalism. Additionally, Kim Jae-young highlights the extremely abusive realities facing those who live on the outskirts of society.

비평의 목소리

Critical Acclaim

첫 소설집 『코끼리』에서부터 김재영은 우리 안의 타자에 대해 남다른 관심을 보여왔다. 아주노동자의 삶을 그리면서도 그는 한국인과 이주노동자를 선악의 선명한 구도로 배치하지 않았고, 성급하게 화해를 시도하거나 어설픈 연대의 포즈를 취하지도 않았다. 그렇다고 이주노동자들의 타락과 부도덕에 초점을 맞춘 것도 아니다. 돈을 모아 고국에 돌아가기 위해 동료의 죽음까지 외면하고 특근을 하던 '노랭이'도, 그 노랭이의 돈을 훔치기 위해 강도로 돌변한 '비재 아저씨'도 실은 "뭐든 집어삼킬 태세로 거세게 휘돌아"가는 '외'에 빠진 코끼리라는 사실을 드러냄으로써 김재영은 바로 저 '외'와도

From her first collection of short stories, *The Elephant*, Kim Jae-young has shown a keen interest in the outsider within us. When depicting the life of migrant laborers Kim does not separate them from native Koreans in terms of good and evil. Kim also does not attempt any sort of hasty reconciliation between the two, nor does she settle for unconvincing bonds of solidarity. This is not to say she has only focused on corruption and unethical behavior in the migrant population. For example, Weaselface does not show up to his coworker's funeral and works overtime to save up for his trip back home. Mr. Vijay turns into a thief to steal

같은 우리의 현실을 문제 삼았다.

이선우

「코끼리」에서 이주노동자는 어떤 정신적인 가치를 지
닌 숭고한 희생자로 등장하지 않고, 자본제의 모순을
비판하기 위해 연대하지도 않는다. 도리어 그들은 자본
제의 '외'에서 혼자만이라도 탈출하기 위해 동료의 돈을
훔치기까지 하는 이기적인 인간들이다. 막내아들의 수
술비를 파키스탄 출신 동료 노동자 '알리'에게 도둑맞은
'비재' 역시 동료 '나딤 몰라'의 돈을 훔친다. 또 이 소설
은 화자로 이주노동자들의 자녀를 등장시키기 때문에
이주노동자들의 문화는 미화되지 않고 그들의 궁핍한
현실은 가능한 핍진하게 그려진다.

김남혁

외국인 이주노동자를 다룬 다른 소설들과 달리 김재
영의 소설에서 주목해야 할 것은 외국인 이주노동자의
주체적 시각에서 예의 문제들이 탐구되고 있다는 점이
다. 비록 그들은 외국에서 이주해온 타자로서 존재하지
만, 그들도 엄연히 한국의 생산관계 속에서 그 몫을 다

104

Weaselface's money. Kim reveals the fact that both of them are elephants caught in a whirlpool that swallows everything in its path, raising issue, instead, with the whirlpool that is our reality.

Lee Seon-u

In "The Elephant," the migrant worker is not depicted as some noble victim of spiritual value. Nor does the story bond with the worker to criticize capitalism's contradictions. Instead, they are selfish humans who steal from coworkers to escape capitalism's whirlpool. It is no surprise that Mr. Vijay steals from his coworker Nadiim Mola, after Ali robs Mr. Vijay of his entire savings for his youngest son's surgery. Also, since this story uses a migrant worker child as the narrator, the culture of the laborers is not beautified. Their destitute realities are shown as is.

Kim Nam-hyeok

Unlike other literature on migrant workers, Kim Jae-young's short story deserves attention for delving into issues of courtesy from a subjective perspective. As migrants from foreign countries, they live as outsiders in Korea. Kim Jae-young,

하고 있기 때문에 한국사회를 구성하고 있는 주체라는 점에 김재영은 주목하고 있다. 하여 그들은 김재영의 소설에서 주체의 지위를 당당히 확보한다. 이것은 외국인 이주노동자의 문제를 다루는 데 중요한 참조점을 제공한다. 지금까지 외국인 이주노동자의 문제에 초점을 맞춘 대부분의 소설들이 한국사회의 소수적 타자로서 겪는 문제들에 대한 나름대로의 해결을 모색하려고 했으나, 그것은 어디까지나 그들을 타자의 경계 안에 가둬놓은 상태에서 한국사회의 보살핌을 받아야 할 사회적 약자라는 점에 초점을 맞추었다. (…) 하지만 김재영은 외국인 이주노동자에 대해 이러한 식민의 시각을 취하지 않는다. 외국인 이주노동자가 '지금, 이곳'에서 겪고 있는 온갖 사회적 차별을 한국사회의 소수적 타자라는 관점으로만 국한시키지 않고, 그들도 한국사회의 노동자란 주체적 지위에서 한국 노동의 부정적 현실을 직시하도록 한다.

고명철

however, focuses on the fact that they actually make up a vital part of Korean society along with a part in Korea's production labor relations force. As such, they secure their place as main agents in Kim's novel. This provides an important point of reference for dealing with the problems facing migrant workers. Most novels focusing on this issue have tried to offer solutions to the problems facing minority migrant workers in Korea. Minority characters are confined within the boundaries of the outsider, perceived as second-rate citizens requiring the care and attention of larger society. [...] Kim Jae-young, on the other hand, does not take this colonial perspective. Instead of limiting migrant worker discrimination to a viewpoint that sees them as minorities, Kim presents them as major agents in society, thereby forcing the reader to confront the negative realities of labor work and life in Korea.

Ko Myeong-cheol

김재영

김재영은 1967년 경기도 여주에서 태어났다. 초등학교 고학년이 되어 서울 쌍문초등학교로 전학 온 뒤, 도봉여중, 송곡여고를 다녔다. 송곡여고 시절에는 '문예반'에 들어가 문학에 대한 공부와 창작을 했다. 1985년 성균관대학교 가정관리학과에 입학했다. 대학생활 내내 학과공부보다는 연극 동아리 '성균극회'에서 극예술에 관심을 가졌다. 대학 3학년이었던 1987년에 전국적으로 불붙은 '6월 항쟁' 시기를 거치면서 사회적 문제의식이 깊어졌다. 이후 생활과학대학 학생회장으로 당선되어 총학생회 운영위원을 겸하면서 열심히 일했다. 학생회 활동이 원인이 되어 학교에서 제적된 뒤, '전국 노점상 연합회' 간사, 성수동 공단 노동자로 취업해 일을 했다. 아들 둘을 낳고 나서 서른한 살 다소 늦은 나이에 '무슨 일을 하고 살면 후회하지 않을 것인가' 진지하게 고민했다. 그때 얻은 답이 '소설'이었다. 자기 삶의 주인이 되고 동시대를 이해하고 사랑하는 방법이라 여겨졌다. 1998년 처음 쓴 소설로 '전태일문학상'에서 입선했

Kim Jae-young

Born in 1967 in Yeoju, Gyeonggi-do, Kim Jae-young moved to Seoul in her later elementary school years and attended Ssangmun Elementary, Dobong Girls Middle School and Songgok Girls High School. While still only in high school, she studied and wrote her own literature. In 1985, she entered SungKyunKwan University and majored in Family Management. During her college years, she took more interest in theatre arts than in her course studies, actively participating in the school's theatre club. It was in her junior year when the Great Workers' Struggle of June 1987 erupted that her social consciousness deepened. She was soon elected as class president of the College of Life Sciences and also worked hard as a member of the Student Council Committee. After her expulsion from school for her activities in student government, she was hired as an assistant administrator for the National Federation of Street Vendors of Korea, located in the Seongsu-dong industrial complex.

다. 이후 1999년 중앙대학교 전문가과정을 수료, 2000년에는 「또 다른 계절」로 《내일을 여는 작가》 제1회 신인상을 받았다. 이후 중단편 소설을 꾸준히 발표하다가 2004년 『코끼리』를 《창작과비평》에 발표해 관심을 받았다. 2005년 창작집 『코끼리』(실천문학사)를 출간했다. 2006년, 중앙대학교 대학원에 입학했다. 2007년 여름부터 1년간 뉴욕의 컬럼비아대학 교환교수로 가게 된 남편과 함께 미국에서 생활했다. 그 시기에 국내외에서 만난 '디아스포라'의 삶을 소설로 썼다. 2009년 창작집 『폭식』(창비)을 출간했다. 2013년 문학박사학위를 받았으며, 현재는 중앙대학교, 명지대학교, 숭의여대에서 문학을 강의하고 있다. '유토피아'를 꿈꾸었던 사람들의 사랑과 배신을 다룬 새 장편소설을 쓰고 있다.

When she was 30, as the mother of two sons, she began to seriously consider how to live a life without regret. The answer was writing. She felt it would allow her to take ownership of her life and understand and love the era she was part of. She wrote her first story in 1998, which won the Jeon Tae-il Literary Award. In 1999, she completed the professionals course at Chungang University, after which she won the *Writers of Tomorrow* New Writer Award for her work, "Another Season." She kept writing short and medium length stories and began to receive critical attention when "The Elephant" was published in *the Quarterly Changbi* in 2004. One year later, her short story collection entitled *The Elephant* (Silcheon Publishing Co.) hit the shelves.

In 2006, she was accepted into Chungang University Graduate School. She then followed her husband to New York in the summer of 2007 for his visiting professorship at Columbia University for one year. During that period, she wrote a novel about life in the diaspora that she encountered there. Her collection, *Gluttony* (Changbi Publishers, Inc.), was published in 2009. She received her doctorate degree in 2013 and is currently teaching literature at Chungang University, Myongji University, and Soongeui Women's College. She is working on a new full-length novel about the love and betrayals of people who once dreamed of a "utopia."

번역 **미셸 주은 김** Translated by Michelle Jooeun Kim

미셸 주은 김(김주은)은 버지니아 주립대학교 국제학과를 졸업하고 한동대학교 통역번역대학원에서 석사학위를 받았다. 이승우 단편소설 「칼」의 번역으로 한국문학번역원 제11회 한국문학번역신인상을 수상하였다.

Michelle Jooeun Kim studied Foreign Affairs at the University of Virginia and received her master's degree in Applied Linguistics and Translation at Handong University's Graduate School of Interpretation and Translation. She received the 11th Korean Literature Translation Award for New Translators with Lee Seung-u's short story "The Knife."

감수 **전승희** Edited by Jeon Seung-hee

전승희는 서울대학교와 하버드대학교에서 영문학과 비교문학으로 박사 학위를 받았으며, 현재 하버드대학교 한국학 연구소의 연구원으로 재직하며 아시아 문예 계간지 《ASIA》 편집위원으로 활동 중이다. 현대 한국문학 및 세계문학을 다룬 논문을 다수 발표했으며, 바흐친의 「장편소설과 민중언어」, 제인 오스틴의 「오만과 편견」 등을 공역했다. 1988년 한국여성연구소의 창립과 《여성과 사회》의 창간에 참여했고, 2002년부터 보스턴 지역 피학대 여성을 위한 단체인 '트랜지션하우스' 운영에 참여해 왔다. 2006년 하버드대학교 한국학 연구소에서 '한국 현대사와 기억'을 주제로 한 워크숍을 주관했다.

Jeon Seung-hee is a member of the Editorial Board of *ASIA*, and a Fellow at the Korea Institute, Harvard University. She received a Ph.D. in English Literature from Seoul National University and a Ph.D. in Comparative Literature from Harvard University. She has presented and published numerous papers on modern Korean and world literature. She is also a co-translator of Mikhail Bakhtin's *Novel and the People's Culture* and Jane Austen's *Pride and Prejudice*. She is a founding member of the Korean Women's Studies Institute and of the biannual Women's Studies' journal *Women and Society* (1988), and she has been working at 'Transition House,' the first and oldest shelter for battered women in New England. She organized a workshop entitled "The Politics of Memory in Modern Korea" at the Korea Institute, Harvard University, in 2006. She also served as an advising committee member for the Asia-Africa Literature Festival in 2007 and for the POSCO Asian Literature Forum in 2008.

바이링궐 에디션 한국 대표 소설 049
코끼리

2014년 3월 7일 초판 1쇄 발행
2024년 8월 14일 초판 4쇄 발행

지은이 김재영 | **옮긴이** 미셸 주은 김 | **펴낸이** 김재범
감수 전승희 | **기획** 정은경, 전성태, 이경재
편집 정수인, 이은혜 | **관리** 박신영 | **디자인** 이춘희
펴낸곳 (주)아시아 | **출판등록** 2006년 1월 27일 제406-2006-000004호
주소 경기도 파주시 회동길 445(서울 사무소: 서울특별시 동작구 서달로 161-1, 3층)
전화 02.3280.5058 | **팩스** 070.7611.2505 | **홈페이지** www.bookasia.org
ISBN 979-11-5662-002-0 (set) | 979-11-5662-006-8 (04810)
값은 뒤표지에 있습니다.

Bi-lingual Edition Modern Korean Literature 049
The Elephant

Written by Kim Jae-young | **Translated by** Michelle Jooeun Kim
Published by Asia Publishers

Address 445, Hoedong-gil, Paju-si, Gyeonggi-do, Korea
(Seoul Office: 161-1, Seodal-ro, Dongjak-gu, Seoul, Korea)

Homepage Address www.bookasia.org | **Tel**. (822).3280.5058 | **Fax**. 070.7611.2505
First published in Korea by Asia Publishers 2014
ISBN 979-11-5662-002-0 (set) | 979-11-5662-006-8 (04810)

바이링궐 에디션 한국 대표 소설

한국문학의 가장 중요하고 첨예한 문제의식을 가진 작가들의 대표작을 주제별로 선정!
하버드 한국학 연구원 및 세계 각국의 한국문학 전문 번역진이 참여한 번역 시리즈!
미국 하버드대학교와 컬럼비아대학교 동아시아학과, 캐나다 브리티시컬럼비아대학교 아시아
학과 등 해외 대학에서 교재로 채택!

바이링궐 에디션 한국 대표 소설 set 1

바이링궐 에디션 한국 대표 소설 set 2

바이링궐 에디션 한국 대표 소설 set 7

백치가 된 식민지 지식인 Colonial Intellectuals Turned "Idiots"

한국의 잃어버린 얼굴 Traditional Korea's Lost Faces

해방 전후(前後) Before and After Liberation

전후(戰後) Korea After the Korean War

K-픽션 시리즈 | Korean Fiction Series

〈K-픽션〉 시리즈는 한국문학의 젊은 상상력입니다. 최근 발표된 가장 우수하고 흥미로운 작품을 엄선하여 출간하는 〈K-픽션〉은 한국문학의 생생한 현장을 국내외 독자들과 실시간으로 공유하고자 기획되었습니다. 〈바이링궐 에디션 한국 대표 소설〉 시리즈를 통해 검증된 탁월한 번역진이 참여하여 원작의 재미와 품격을 최대한 살린 〈K-픽션〉 시리즈는 매 계절마다 새로운 작품을 선보입니다.